THE
HEART
PEN

Judi Taylor

Cover design by Susan Larned Womble

ISBN: 978-0-578-71884-2
First Edition

Printed in the United States of America

           ISBN: 978-0-578-71884-2

ACKNOWLEDGEMENTS

I thank my husband, Darrell, for supporting this book endeavor, and for sharing my life. He makes me feel special every day. *I love our journey, and I love you!* I thank my sister, Susan, for all her inspiration and mentoring for this book, and in my life! She has been my best friend since day one and has always been there for me. *I love you!* I give a special shout out to the rest of my beautiful family. You have added to my life in every way. *I feel very blessed!*

PROLOGUE
JUNE 2, 1990

As most people do on their birthday, I am thinking back over the accomplishments of my 28 years on this earth. I finished college, became a teacher, and married the man of my dreams. To top it all off, I had a beautiful baby girl last year who has become the center of our life. I usually think of my birthday as a day to reflect and to look forward to the future. But today I will only be reflecting. The doctors say that my cancer has spread to my heart and I don't have much time left. My name is Sophie Walsh, formerly Sophie Garcia. My grandparents migrated to America from Spain many years ago. They opened a Spanish restaurant that was passed down to my parents. Most of my childhood years were spent helping around the restaurant and welcoming the guests. The regulars watched me grow up and became an extension of my family.

I have always been thankful for my Spanish descent. I was blessed with long, luxurious black hair, dark eyes, and olive skin. I considered my slight accent as sort of a romantic trait that set me apart from the Americans. My husband, Tom Walsh, seemed to agree. Tom is of Irish descent and has the red hair and green eyes to prove it. We are total opposites in our appearance, but alike in our values and goals. And after three years of marriage, he still remains the sweetest man I have ever met.

I am sitting in a comfy white wicker chair in our sunroom surrounded by pure white lilies, my favorite flower. I think back to the week that we moved into this house. Tom and I planted a few of the lilies, envisioning them as decoration for a romantic little hide-a-way. They surprised us by multiplying quickly and now they form a thick lining against the three glass walls of the room. Hundreds of white lilies are in full bloom as I gaze across the room today. I cannot imagine a more spectacular spot than the one where I am sitting. I have spent many hours in this spot since the day Dr. Dunn told me that my days on this earth were numbered. It seems that the same heart that has brought me so much love and joy is now ending it all. I have been trying to come to terms with my fate, as well as trying to prepare my husband for the day that he will become a single parent to a small baby. He has his mother and a sister nearby, so I know he will make it through. *I need to keep positive thoughts!*

As for Lily, my precious little girl named for my favorite flower, I find myself crying continuously over all the things I will miss in her life. Tom will be a wonderful father (*back to thinking of the positives!*). He can teach her to be a strong, independent young woman. Tom's sister, Cindy, is very caring and loving, so I can count on her to help guide my Lily's feminine side. Sitting here looking at the sea of white lilies transports my mind to thoughts of Lily's wedding day. I kept my wedding dress in a storage bag, just in case Lily ever wanted to see it. So, now, in my visions of the future she is always wearing my dress. It makes me feel good to dream about her wanting to feel my presence. I can see Tom looking handsome as he walks her down the aisle. I pray that she chooses a good man with whom to share her life. And, in my mind she is the most beautiful bride ever. I would so much like to be there to share the moment. I would tell her how wonderful a true love can be and how much I love her father. We would share our dreams and goals. I can see the look of happiness in her eyes and my love for her shining bright in the reflection. What a proud mother I would be! But instead, I am sitting here with tears streaming down and wetting everything in sight. Tom comes out to join me in the sunroom. No doubt he has heard my crying, and I feel so sad for him.

"What are you thinking about?" he asks.

"I was just imagining our Lily's wedding day." I try to sound happy when I describe it but know that I am not fooling him.

His eyes brighten as an idea forms. "You should write her a letter to be opened on her wedding day!" he declares, "It can be your gift to her."

I sit and mull this thought over. I wonder if this is something that I can do. Could I capture my thoughts and feelings on paper? I tell him that I will think about it and then it becomes *all* that I can think about. The next day I wake up with more hope than I have felt in quite a while. I have decided to write the letter to Lily, and it gives my day a purpose. With more energy than I've had in months, I rummage around to find some beautiful notepaper that I know we had left over from our wedding. I finally find it tucked away in my top drawer. As my mind jumps forward to finding a pen, my eyes glance down at my jewelry box. I open it and spy the pen covered with red hearts. My memory flashes back to the first Valentine's Day after Tom and I met. We were poor college students, so we celebrated with a pizza and beer at our favorite spot. Tom declared that I deserved a gift on this special night. While I was disagreeing, he walked over and put change into the

"Claw" game, the one that slowly lowers a big claw while you navigate it to scoop up the perfect prize. He was definitely going for the clear box with the giant bauble ring in it, but the claw fell clumsily to its side. Tom's face registered such disappointment that I couldn't help but laugh! But, as the claw began to rise, we noticed that it had clasped around a bigger clear box. I remember how excited Tom was when he saw that it held an ink pen covered in red hearts. He was so proud of that gift! I will never forget the love I felt as he presented it to me and called me his Valentine.

This memory has filled my heart and lightened my mood. With pen and paper in hand, I realize this is the perfect time to write a letter to my dear Lily.

CHAPTER 1
AUGUST 2002
LILY

I wake up and my first thought is that school starts next week – ugh! This is my last week of summer vacation. I hear dad in the kitchen, so I join him and am happy to see him heaping scrambled eggs onto a platter.

"I thought it was about time for you to get up," he says, a little too cheery for this early in the morning. "Are you ready for breakfast?"

I shake my head and plop down at the table. He fills our plates with eggs, bacon, and a biscuit before joining me at the table. He is already dressed for work so I know our breakfast will be quick. "Do you have a busy day?" I ask, trying to judge how late he'll be back. My dad owns an insurance agency and doesn't always work the normal 8-5 hours.

"Yes, it's busy this morning, but I should be able to get home around 3:00. Do you want to drive down to the lake later and do a little fishing?"

"Yes!" I answer with all the energy I can muster this early.

"Luckily, Kathryn will be back tomorrow, so this should be your last day alone." Dad says. Kathryn is my cousin and my best friend. She is two years older than me and seems to always have answers to my questions. Dad bought a house next door to his sister, Cindy, when my mother died a long time ago. Aunt Cindy and Uncle Bob have always included me as part of their family. I didn't go with them on this trip since they were visiting Uncle Bob's brother. They have only been gone a couple of days, but I've been pretty lonely without them.

"What are you going to do today?" Dad asks.

"I'm going to start by giving Beau some exercise," I announce. Beau is our golden retriever and my trustee companion on lonely days. "I bought him a new toy when Aunt Cindy took me shopping for school clothes. I'll show you!" I say as I jump up and walk toward my room.

"Oh, Lily!" Dad exclaims as I get to my door.

I turn to see a weird look on his lightly flushed face. Sudden worry comes over me. "What is it, Dad?"

"Uh… there's something on your pajama bottoms. Have you hurt yourself in any way?" he asks.

"No, what is it?" I ask while trying to twist my pants around.

"Uh, this could be what Aunt Cindy told you would happen when your body starts transitioning into a woman."

"Ugh" I grunt as I run to the bathroom. I sit down on the toilet and am shocked. What a mess! Emotion slowly overcomes me. How could I not have felt this? Where is Aunt Cindy when I need her? Why can't I have a mom? Tears start flowing as I fully succumb to feeling sorry for myself. Dad jolts me out of my trance as he gently raps on the door.

"Are you OK, honey?"

I can tell how concerned he is, so I pull myself together. "Yes, Dad… I am fine. I think it is my womanhood calling." I answer jokingly to ease his concern.

"Do you remember everything Aunt Cindy told you? Do you need anything?" he asks with worry in his voice.

I answer a little too quickly, "All is fine. I have it covered. Have a great day at work." But I am not fine. Why couldn't Dad have remarried? I would at least have a stepmom. I throw off my pajamas and step into the shower. Life is so unfair – and now this! I stand under the warm water and finish crying out all my tears. I sob until there is no more, and then I feel calmer and start trying to deal with my situation. I remember Aunt Cindy giving me a book to explain everything in detail, and a box of pads to keep on hand. I dry off quickly and rummage through the linen closet to find the book and pads. I grab clean underwear and follow the diagram on the box. At least that was easy. I pull out my baggiest shorts to put on and finish getting dressed. Then I spread out on the bed and read the entire book.

When I finish, I feel totally alone and depressed. I think about how wonderful it would be to have a mother. Dad tries hard and I love him so much, but it's just not the same. Aunt Cindy has always been there for me and I am so thankful for her. But still, I see the mother/daughter bond that she and Kathryn have, and I cannot help but be jealous.

I go to my closet and pull out the only link I have to my mother... her wedding dress. I unzip the storage bag and pull it out. It is, and always has been, the most beautiful dress there ever was. I go to Dad's room and retrieve the only picture I have ever seen of my mother. The picture was taken after their wedding ceremony. They are posing in front of the cake and Mom is looking up at Dad. Dad and Aunt Cindy say that I look just like my mom with my long black hair and olive coloring, except for the green eyes that I inherited from Dad. In the picture, Mom's hair is pinned up with her veil covering most of it. She is turned and smiling up at Dad, so I can't even see her full face. But she is wearing this dress – the dress in my hands that I can touch and know that it has touched my mother. The dress is made of delicate white lace with a white shiny lining under it. It has a pale pink ribbon around the waist. The sleeves are long and made of lace. I look at the picture and see Mom's dark arms peeking out of the lace and think of how feminine she looks. I try to picture myself wearing this dress someday, but do not ever see myself as pretty as her. I shake myself back to reality, gently put away the dress, and close my pity party. I grab Beau's dog toy and go out to exercise us both.

I act as though nothing has happened when Dad gets home. I can tell that he is happy with not having to discuss it. We go to the lake and enjoy an afternoon of fishing. I go to bed early knowing that Kathryn is coming back tomorrow.

The next morning, I sleep through breakfast and wake to hear Dad leaving for work. I jump up and shower, and then sit on the porch and watch for Uncle Bob's car. It finally comes and Kathryn runs over as soon as she gets out of the car. I listen to a few of her travel stories before sharing my secret. "Why didn't you warn me that it would be so gross?" I demand.

"I didn't want to scare you. You get used to it after a few months." She is always so sensible. "And, now you are a woman. You could actually have children now!" she says with a smile.

"This is supposed to be GOOD news? Kathryn, you know that I am never going to have kids. I'm afraid that I would have one and then die or leave it somehow. I wouldn't wish that on any child."

Kathryn is always appalled when I say this and always answers it the same way. "Oh, you'll change your mind when you grow up and fall in love. I plan to have at least four kids, and maybe more. And, we'll have a beautiful little house with a big yard and a dog."

Since I have heard this conversation more than once, I suggest that we walk down to the convenience store and buy some candy. We spend the rest of our day looking through our new clothes and talking about the upcoming school year.

As I lay down that night, my head swims with thoughts of being a woman, a new school year, the wedding dress… until I drift off to sleep.

CHAPTER 2
16 YEARS LATER
LILY

It is a bright sunny day as I make my last trip up to Thomasville for the final fitting of my wedding dress. I am taking an extra thirty minutes for my lunch break so I can get this task completed. It is two weeks until the wedding. The planning has exhausted me, and I am ready for it to be here.

My thoughts turn to my Mom, and I feel a quick pain of sorrow that she will not be at my wedding. It has always bothered me that my Mom died before my first birthday and I never got the chance to know her. I hate the jealous feelings I get when I see my friends with their moms, and I admit to having a little chip on my shoulder about the whole thing. When I was growing up and needed a mom, I would always pull out her wedding picture and wedding dress. It didn't help much, but it was all I had. And now, I will be wearing that same dress at my wedding next week. I have always known that I would wear her dress. I started trying it on as soon as I was big enough to fill out some of it, just waiting to fit into it. It's a wonder that the dress is still in such beautiful shape, but I admit to treating it as my most precious possession.

I am jarred back into the present as I arrive at Elaine's Alteration Shop. I park easily since Elaine runs a small Shop and only schedules one client at a time. I walk toward the shop in the sweltering heat of the day, trying not to sweat before trying on my dress.

"Hi!" says Elaine, as I enter the shop and see my dress hanging beside her. "I'm ready for you. Your big day is getting so close. Are you nervous?"

I laugh and say, "There is no time to be nervous. There is so much to do! I'm going to go ahead and slip on the dress, if that's OK?"

Elaine agrees and waits quietly until I emerge from the dressing room a few minutes later. "Ah-h, stunning!" she says as I move to the front of the mirror.

I nod and say, "Yes, I'm lucky that my mother had such good taste. I don't like most of the styles these days, and I have always loved vintage clothes."

Elaine had only made two changes to my Mom's dress. She cut the long sleeves off above the elbow. I didn't think I could handle them at a June wedding in Florida, even if they were made from lace. She also had to take the dress in at the waist and hips a bit. My Mom must have had a curvier shape than I do. Looking in the mirror, I see that the dress now perfectly fits my thinner shape.

"Elaine, thank you so much. This dress now looks as if it was made just for me. And, this is the one thing I have not had to worry about during all this planning. You are the best!"

I can see that Elaine is happy to hear the compliments, and they are well deserved. I change back into my work clothes, and she hangs the dress in a plastic bag while I finish paying my bill. I thank her again and ask if she will be at the wedding next week.

"I wouldn't miss it," she says. "I will be so proud to see you in that dress."

I leave feeling thrilled that I have one more thing to check off my list. On the drive back to work, I think about how much I have left to do. I also think about Kyle, the wonderful man with whom I have chosen to share the rest of my life. He has such a gentle spirit and an uplifting attitude on life.

I am generally happy, but I admit that the "chip on my shoulder" comes out sometimes when I least expect it. I think back over my happy life. My Dad was always there for me and Aunt Cindy was always there to help. Kathryn and I grew up like sisters. We shared everything and know all each other's deepest secrets. But, even so, I always felt a void in my heart, in the place where my mother's love was missing. I try not to dwell on it because I end up feeling sorry for myself, which raises my defenses. I do not like this quality about myself but have never had any luck in changing it.

But Kyle seems to know me better than I know myself. When I slip into one of these moods, he quickly changes the subject in such a way that I fall out of the mood before I even realize it. I love that about him. Rather than fight with me or let me feel sorry for myself, he just quickly moves on to happier subjects. When we started discussing where we would live after the wedding, I insisted on my apartment even though it was smaller, because it was much more charming. He wanted us to live in his larger apartment which was also less expensive. I immediately fell into my "poor pitiful" mode and said I couldn't understand why I had to be the one to move. Kyle, in his loving way, pointed out that his was bigger, cheaper, and closer to my job. He said it just needed a woman's touch and I was free to decorate as I saw fit, but to keep in mind that a man was also living there. Argument avoided! Thinking about Kyle puts a smile on my face as I enter the parking lot of Walter & Johnson Associates, the CPA firm where I have been employed for the last five years. I have an appointment scheduled with one of my clients, so the afternoon flies by.

I rush home after work and change into more casual clothes. Then, I start packing up the remaining items in the room that has served as my office. I am saddened at the thought of leaving this apartment that I have rented for the past six years. I moved in when I finished college, so I will always think of it as my first home as a grown up. My bedroom reflects my feminine side with pale yellow walls and lavender bedding. And I always keep a lily on the bedside table. My dad told me that I was named after the lily flower, so that immediately became my trademark.

I fill my car with as many of the packed boxes as it will hold and drive to Kyle's apartment. I have already given notice that I will vacate my apartment by June 16th, so I am slowly moving all my belongings into Kyle's apartment. Since his is bigger, most of my things will fit easily. Gone are the days of lavender bedspreads, but Kyle's bedroom is decorated in a bold turquoise and brown and the combination has really grown on me. He agrees that my lilies will be a fine addition to his barren looking dining table and that I can always keep one at my bedside.

The drive over is short, and Kyle is cooking dinner when I arrive. "Um-m-m," I say as I walk in carrying a box. "Something smells delicious!"

He takes the box and gives me a quick peck on the cheek. "I'm cooking red sauce, so I hope you're in the mood for spaghetti. I'll help you unload boxes while it simmers."

I take him up on the offer since he can lift so much more than me. He has them all inside in a matter of minutes and I help move them into his second bedroom.

He uses it as an office, and he has cleared half of the room for me. Kyle finishes cooking while I unpack and start setting up my side of the office. It is not long before he calls me for dinner, and I follow the aroma. We fill our plates and sit at his table.

"I picked up my dress today," I say in a sing song.

"I can't wait to see it! Actually, I can't wait until all of this is over and we can begin our life together."

We chat easily about the wedding, catching up on all that has been done and all that still needs to be done. I head back to my apartment early to finish packing a few more things to move over the weekend.

The following week passes by quickly. On Saturday morning I wake up feeling well rested. I put on running clothes and head out into the beautiful morning. I smile as I finish my four-mile jog. It has had such a calming effect and I am ready to face the day. I enter the house and hear the phone ringing. I know immediately that the calm won't last long!

"Lily, I'm going to be a few minutes late for lunch," Kathryn says. "Sorry! I was late finishing up at the nail salon. I left Jacksonville a few minutes ago, though, so I'm on my way!"

"No problem," I say. "We will sip our Mimosas until you arrive. Drive carefully!" I'm smiling as I hang up. I haven't seen Kathryn in a couple of months and I always miss her when we're apart. We were inseparable until she graduated and left to attend a fashion school in Atlanta. Then, she landed a job as a buyer for Nordstrom stores in Jacksonville and has been there ever since. We are still as close as any sisters and I'm looking forward to seeing her later today.

I shower and put on my new Lilly Pulitzer halter dress that I bought last week. The bright colors make me smile. I paid more than I usually do for a dress, but I knew it would be perfect for this bridesmaid's luncheon and to take on the honeymoon cruise. I arrive at the restaurant to see two of the bridesmaids being led to a table outside on the deck, so I catch up to them. As we are seated, I tell them that Kathryn is running late. "So, let's start with Mimosas!" I say to the waiter as he walks up.

The drinks arrive and Melody toasts, "Many more happy moments to Lily, the bride-to-be!" We all clink our glasses in agreement. Melody is my best friend from college. She has bright red hair and dancing blue eyes. When she smiles, her whole face exudes a happiness that is infectious. She has never worn make-up and has always carried extra weight, but her confidence makes her beautiful! We both lived in a scholarship house and roomed together all four years at Florida State University. We were total opposites in many ways. I chose accounting because of my love for numbers and equations. Melody had grown up in a family that lived for music (hence the name Melody!). They were all musically inclined and so talented. Melody can light up a room with her piano playing and singing. I sometimes thought of how boring it made my number-crunching sound, but I must admit to being an accounting nerd.

Melody is now a music professor at FSU. As opposite as our career choices were in college, we shared a common interest in doing our part to make the world a better place (or at least our community!). Even in college, we always made time to volunteer at several of the non-profit centers in Tallahassee. It served as a good reminder to us that the world was much larger than our campus and our small circle of friends. I still try to squeeze in time to volunteer at the local food bank when

I can, but Melody has never wavered from her commitment to help others. She volunteers at an after-school music program at one of the local middle schools and has formed a singing group for under-privileged girls. She says the reward is in discovering their hidden talent and seeing the girls develop pride in themselves.

The other bridesmaid seated with us is Ella, and she happily toasts "To Lily's wedding and to what I hope will be the biggest social event of the year!" We laugh and clink our glasses again. Ella is Kyle's younger sister and will soon be my new sister-in-law. She and Kyle favor each other and are both very striking. Kyle has dark hair and bright blue eyes and is ruggedly handsome. Ella has the same bright blue eyes and has curly blond hair that has been cropped short for as long as I've known her. She is thin and athletic, which gives her a tomboyish look. She and Kyle grew up in Tallahassee and both attended FSU. Kyle is a lawyer now and Ella works for the Tallahassee newspaper. She covers all the local happenings, including the wedding announcements and obituaries. We know that she is hoping for some excitement to write about at the wedding, but I am hoping for a low-key celebration that goes just as planned!

After a few minutes of chatting, we see Kathryn's confident stride as she makes her way to our table. "Check out these beautiful nails," she exclaims. "I know that I'll have them done again for the wedding next weekend, but they looked too bad to wait. I had them painted blue to match this cute little outfit today, but I won't be able to stand blue for too long, so it'll work out." We all admire her soft blue skirt topped with a nautical looking silk tank. She is such a fashionista! And, her curves seem to make every outfit come alive. Her brunette hair hangs perfectly in a long bob style. She has the same green eyes as mine, thanks to our Irish family.

As Kathryn sits, the waiter comes over for our orders. He tells us that the daily special is a salad garnished with strawberries and walnuts. We all order it, being mindful of the dresses we have to fit into next week!

"I can't believe that in one week you will be an old married lady." Kathryn says.

"Well, you and Rick have been married for three years already – so look who's talking!" I reply. I think to myself about Kathryn's dream to get married and start having babies right away. She always said that she would quit work for a few years to stay home with them, but that she would keep in "fashion" practice by turning them into the best dressed babies ever. Rick is a doctor, and he bought right into her plan. But after three unsuccessful years of trying to get pregnant naturally, then by in vitro fertilization, they are finally turning their sights to adoption. None of the testing ever identified any problems. It just seems that it was not meant to be. From our phone conversations, I know that it is taking a toll on them and that finding a baby to adopt has taken over her life. But she has on a happy face today as our meals are served and we discuss the dresses and schedule of events.

"Enough talk about my wedding," I finally say. "What's going on with everybody?"

It's not hard to tell the direction of Melody's passion when she immediately starts talking about her volunteer job. "Did I tell you that my girls have been invited to sing at "Under the Stars?" We all know that she is referring to the Tallahassee Hospital's biggest fundraiser of the year as she has definitely mentioned this more than once!

"Yes, what night is that?" I reply excitedly.

"It's scheduled for Friday, July 13th." she answers. "You all need to put it on your calendar and be sure to buy tickets. Guess who is headlining it?" she asks. We have no idea but hope that it is someone good since we all surely will have to attend. "Nikki Sue!" she almost shouts.

"Really?" we all reply in unison. This excites us as Nikki Sue is currently one of the hottest female singers alive.

"She is my favorite!" Ella declares, "We better buy our tickets soon." We all agree that it will be a sellout, so we each give Ella money to buy all our tickets together.

I remember that last time I talked to Melody she was working on a grant application to continue the funding for her after school singing group. "How is the grant writing going?" I ask.

"I finished it and barely made the submission deadline. Keep your fingers crossed because they should be announcing the winners soon."

I say a silent prayer for her. I know how hard she worked on that grant and how important funding is for the continuation of her program. We all chime "Good luck!"

"Alright, can I turn this into a B*Session?" Ella blurts out. This has become a ritual for us that started off as our Pity Party. It seems that at least one of us always needs an opportunity to openly complain about something in our life. Now we call it our B*Session (use your imagination!) and talk about any problems that we need to get off our chest. It usually helps to minimize the irritation of a situation. And sometimes just saying something out loud helps to let go of a little of the stress.

"OK," I say. "What's wrong, Ella?"

"The same thing that's always wrong in my life! My creative juices are flowing. I write my heart out on my newspaper pieces. But, it's hard to highlight my talents when I'm writing about a small hometown event. And the pay! I'm still trying to save money by living with Mom and Dad, but something always comes up. I had a flat tire last week and ended up having to buy a new set of tires. I can't get a break!"

"Bummer," I say. "It does seem like you get your share of rainy days. Maybe this will be the beginning of a long lucky streak for you. We will all send good thoughts your way! Now, it's my turn to vent. On one hand, I'm getting ready for a beautiful wedding and marrying the man of my dreams. He even agreed to my credo of not having children. But I keep getting more and more depressed about not having a mother to share in this dream come true. You dear friends and Aunt Cindy are the best. But, can any of you imagine how much you would miss your mother? I used to think I only missed having a mother during my sad times. But this is supposed to be the happiest day of my life and I find that I am missing her more than ever."

"Oh-h," says Kathryn. "I remember how wonderful my mom was during my wedding, so I totally understand. I know some things will be hard for you, but we'll try our best to fill in for your mom whenever we can." She smiles and squeezes my hand. "Now, my turn! My problem just seems to be getting worse and worse. Now that we've given up on the in vitro, we're devoting all our spare time to finding a baby to adopt. So far, we've had no success. We're getting to the end of our ropes and we end up arguing over the smallest things these days. We are not in a good place, and we may have to face the possibility of never having children. At this point, maybe we could at least find a way to recapture ourselves as a couple."

"Hang in there," Melody says. "Something good will happen when you least expect it. I just know it will." We all shake our heads in agreement. Melody continues with her turn, "My main complaint right now is the fact that the school or the state won't come through with any funding for my girls' singing group. The politicians talk about wanting to give more opportunities for young girls but won't put any money behind it. My other problem is finding a new dress for the Under the Stars event that will hide my extra 40 pounds! Of course, a date would be nice too."

We all laugh and agree that we feel better after putting our problems out there. After all, that's what good friends are for – sharing our good and bad!

We finish our meals and start saying our goodbyes. Kathryn says that she is heading back to Jacksonville, but that she will be taking Friday off to come back in time for the rehearsal. I remind them that we will meet at 4:00 Friday at the FSU Alumni Center. I have seen pictures of weddings at the Alumni Center and am excited to be having my wedding at such a beautiful venue.

"See you all next Friday. The countdown is ON!" I shout, as we all hug and say our goodbyes. I know that I'll talk to each of them on the phone this week, but we won't meet again until the big event. It makes me nervous as I realize this and wonder if all our plans will come together.

Later that evening, I drive over to my Dad's house. Aunt Cindy is meeting us there to go over the plans one last time. Aunt Cindy brings a fruit and cheese platter and Dad opens a bottle of wine. We sit around the table and everything feels so right. Dad and his sister have loved and supported me through all my years of growing up. We are totally relaxed as we go over every detail. Dad has been a real trooper. I realize that making wedding plans would not be #1 on his list of fun things to do. But he has always tried to be both a mom and dad for me as much as he could. We finish and Aunt Cindy gets up to leave.

"I guess I won't see you again until Friday afternoon, huh?' I ask.

"No" she says, "but I think we're ready. I'll meet you at the Alumni Center around 4:00. Have a good week and don't worry about a thing!" I give her a big bear hug before she leaves for home.

Dad pours us a little more wine and asks me to sit for a few more minutes. He looks serious and this gets my imagination going. I don't think I can cope with any bad news right now. I think wedding plans induce enough emotion by themselves. He moves to the counter and brings a small box over to the table. "I'm not really sure how to approach this," he says. "Maybe we should've discussed it earlier, but the time never seemed right."

"What is it, Dad? Is everything alright?"

He continues as if he hasn't heard me. "Your mother died so long ago. She was a big part of my life, but I realize that you never even got to know her. I've tried to tell you stories throughout your life. I wanted to give you an idea of how wonderful she was and how much she loved you. When she was dying, her greatest sadness was that she wouldn't see you grow up into a young lady and get married." He paused and looked very sad as I peered into his eyes.

"Dad, what is it?"

He took a moment before continuing, and I thought

about how much I loved my dear father. Whatever he was trying to say, I could see the love he had for me in his face.

"Lily, when your mother was very sick, I walked up on her as she sat quietly crying. She told me that she was thinking about your wedding day and how beautiful it would be. It broke my heart, so I suggested that she write a letter to you as a wedding gift. She spent the next couple of days working on the letter. I could see the joy in her eyes as she sat thinking of the perfect words. She finished it and wrapped it in this box. I have no idea what is in here, or how to prepare you for it. I'm giving it to you to take home today in hopes that you will find the perfect time to open it over the next week."

I am so surprised that it takes me a moment to recover myself. "Wow, Dad. I can't believe mom actually wrote me a message." I say as tears well up in my eyes. I try to look calm, but my heart is pounding as I think about my mother talking to me through this letter. I know that I will have to open it sometime when I am alone as I am not sure that I can keep my emotions intact. "Thank you, Dad. I'll take it home and open it when the moment is right."

"Of course." he says, and I can see tears forming in his eyes.

I get up to leave and give him a great big hug. "I love you, Dad. And, you will always be the best dad ever in my heart."

"I love you too, Lily. We have a big week ahead of us, so go home and get some good sleep!"

I get home and exhaustion takes over. My emotions have already been on overload. I dress for bed and decide to leave the box in my purse for now.

The following week goes by smoothly. I check in

with each bridesmaid to be sure everything is going well. I see Kyle several times during the week. I think we are both ready to get through this week and move on to the honeymoon... relaxing on board a luxurious yacht.

We enjoy a nice quiet dinner together on Thursday night, probably our last time alone until after the wedding. Kyle mentions the vows that we have agreed to write to each other. I admit to him that I've been thinking about them but haven't come up with anything, yet. He is excited to tell me that his are finished and I can visibly see his relief. I wonder to myself how I will ever accomplish this task, as I have actually been trying to think of what to say. The more I think about it, the more monumental it becomes. I change the subject by telling him how much I'm looking forward to the rehearsal dinner the following evening. We chat easily about our schedule, and I push the vows to the back of my mind – once again! We both plan to work a half day tomorrow, so we part early and make our plans to meet before the rehearsal.

Once home, I crawl into bed and I am pleasantly surprised when I wake up the next morning and have managed to get a full night of relaxing sleep! I make it through my half day of work, run a few errands, and then head off to the Alumni Center. I am relieved when all the necessary people show up on time. We spend a few minutes ensuring that everyone knows where to enter and where to stand. We run through the entire schedule a couple of times without any problems. This makes us happy, so we all proceed to the rehearsal dinner. Kyle and his parents have planned this at Pierre's, a quaint little French restaurant with a romantic atmosphere. I feel surrounded by love as I look around the room and see our closest friends and relatives. The meal is exquisite, and the conversation stays lively. Travis, Kyle's brother and best man, stands up to make a toast. But he ends up telling a long funny story about the days leading up to Kyle's proposal to me. He became our entertainment and reveled in every minute of it.

The evening goes by quickly and ends with many hugs. I think about how much I've been through with these friends and family – all the ups and downs of life, celebrating one another's accomplishments and sharing each other's disappointments. I start feeling very nostalgic. Tears begin to form as I remember how they have all helped me to get to this point in my life. Whoa, I'm beginning to wonder if I am actually going to make it through this weekend without crying every other minute!

I turn my thoughts toward tonight as I see the trio of bridesmaids rushing toward me. We plan to spend the night together at Melody's house. I am sure that we will stay up too late reminiscing over all the funny stories in our past. I've been looking forward to the opportunity to enjoy one last slumber party as a single woman. Before we head to our cars, I give Kyle a final hug and kiss, and tell him that I'll see him tomorrow at the altar.

We all arrive at Melody's and quickly change into old fashioned pajamas. Melody pours wine as we all sprawl out comfortably on her king-size bed. Then she starts updating us on the upcoming Under the Stars event. "I have been racking my brain to find the perfect song for the girls to sing. No luck, yet, but the event is still a month away. I need to decide soon, though, so they can start practicing. But they did come up with a name for their group! They chose *The Singing Melodies!*" she said with a big smile. "They said they wanted to name it after me as thanks for believing in them. I just love those girls!" We all congratulate her and tell her it really is the perfect name.

Ella takes her cue to say that she would be covering the event that night for the newspaper. "I will make sure to give *The Singing Melodies* plenty of press! Actually, I could also throw in some background information around your forming of the group and the positive changes you've witnessed in the girls." Melody squeals with delight upon hearing this, which makes us all giggle like little schoolgirls.

Kathryn starts telling us about a big fashion show being sponsored by Nordstrom's. They just scheduled it and she has two weeks to choose the outfits and find the models. "But, it's a great chance to showcase some of the new summer styles," she states, and we can all tell that she will enjoy every minute of the busy planning.

Ella brings us back to the wedding again, and says "Lily, I think you are living your dream! I am so happy for you. My dream is to write a book and I haven't even gotten close. I'm not sure I even have a book in me! It may never happen."

Kathryn answers "Well, what about me? This adoption process is beginning to seem just as hard as getting pregnant! I'm not sure how long we can take it before we give up and decide it's just not meant to be. The strain is really starting to get to us."

Melody chimes in "Well, as excited as I am about Under the Stars, I have to acknowledge that this could be the end for my girls and for the whole program. How sad would that be?!

I jump in to remind them that my wedding is tomorrow. "And, I think it will be the beginning of good things for all of us. Our time has got to be coming!

We talk about the rehearsal dinner and how much fun it was to connect with some of our friends that we don't see often. Finally, we talk until we wear ourselves out and slowly drift off to sleep.

I suddenly wake around 1 a.m. It takes me a minute to realize where I am. I must be nervous about our busy day tomorrow. Not tomorrow - I shiver and correct myself as I realize it is already my wedding day. We all have morning appointments at the salon for our nails, hair, and makeup. We'll grab a late lunch, and then retreat to our respective houses to pick up our dresses and accessories. By then it will be about time to meet at the Alumni Center. We will be getting dressed in a small room off to the side of the center. I suddenly remember my vows that I still need to write! I don't know why I've been putting this off, but my mind struggles every time I try to put something in writing. Time is quickly running out, so I will myself to quit stalling. I quietly roll out of bed, grab my purse, and walk into the living room. I start rummaging through my purse to find a pen when I see the small box from my mother. I have carried it around all week, but the time never seemed right to open it. I have actually been too nervous to open it. I stare at the box for a few minutes and decide this may be the perfect time. I realize that this will be my last peace and quiet before the wedding. I curl up on Melody's sofa and turn on the side lamp. Slowly, I untie the ribbon and lift the lid of the box. It contains a letter that is handwritten on beautiful stationary and an ink pen covered with red hearts. I unfold the letter and feel my heart racing. The letter is dated June 2, 1990. I sadly remember that my mother died on July 1, 1990. She was confined to her bed the last several weeks, so this must have been written during one of her last days of mobility. Tears are already beginning to form. I have no idea what to expect since I really never knew my mother. I have heard stories over the years that gave me small glimpses into her personality. But I am overwhelmed by the reality that I am holding something that contains her actual thoughts. Nervously, I start to read.

My Dearest Daughter,

I am sitting in our little sunroom surrounded by lily flowers. This is my favorite place as it provides me with a feeling of inner peace. You are sleeping soundly on a blanket beside me with the sweetest expression on your face. I look down at you and feel more love than I ever thought was possible. I glance around at all the lily flowers that were the inspiration for your name. After we decided on your name, I read somewhere that the word Lily symbolized purity of heart and refined beauty. I knew it was the perfect choice.

I want you to know how much your dad and I loved each other. After we were married, I thought of myself as the luckiest girl in the world. I loved the life we shared and the simple things that we enjoyed together. We both love to cook so the kitchen provides us with time to catch up on each other's day. We are both fierce competitors at tennis, and as double partners we are hard to beat! We love to take long walks or bicycle rides on sunny days, and then relax out here in our lily room. We thought that we were the happiest we could ever be until the day you arrived. You changed our lives and completed us in every way. You made our life perfect.

I am saddened when I think of all the things that I will miss in your life. But I know with certainty that you will be happy. I can feel it in my heart. This thought helps me to get through each day. And, I don't want you ever to be sad when you think of me. My life has been cut short, but I want you to always know that I had a lifetime of love and happiness packed into it – thanks to you and your dad.

I wanted to send this special note for your wedding day. I hope that you have found your true love. I pray that you will build a perfect life together and enjoy many years of happiness. I don't have to be there to know that you are the most beautiful bride to ever walk down that aisle; I can see it in my mind. And, I know your father will look handsome as he proudly walks down that aisle with you.

I hope you will feel my love for you. I will always be looking down from above. I will see your smile as you brighten the room, and I will be beaming. Always remember that you are the very best thing I ever did in my life.

I love you with all my heart,

Mom

I hold the letter closely and cry silently for a few minutes. I cry for the mother I never got to know and for the things we never got to share. But the letter makes me feel a special closeness to her that I've never experienced before. I have been able to hear her thoughts from a time when I was right beside her – while she was looking at me! Dad has told me many stories about how happy they were during their brief time together, but this letter brought me into the picture. What a magnificent gift my mother has given me on my wedding day.

I am beaming as I carefully refold the letter and reach for the box. The heart covered pen is shining up at me, so I take it out and delicately place the letter back in the box and close the lid. I am still reeling in my mother's love as I clutch the pen, when I suddenly remember the vows that I should be writing. I try to concentrate as I fish some paper from my purse. I lean up to the coffee table with my heart pen in hand and the words leap from my mind. They keep flowing until I realize that I am finished with my vows in a matter of minutes. I read back over them, and to my surprise, I have captured the perfect words to convey my feelings to my new husband. I am astonished at how easily they came upon my heart. I feel like a weight has been lifted as I lean back on the sofa to soak in the moment.

The next thing I know, I hear a noise in the kitchen and can smell a fresh pot of coffee brewing. I glance at the clock and am shocked to see that it is 7 a.m. and I am still on the sofa. I startle Melody as I call out to her.

"When did you get up?" she asks. She pours us coffee while I tell her about getting my vows written. I decide not to mention my mom's letter just yet, wanting to keep it close to my heart for now. For the first time, I am feeling giddy with excitement and am ready to begin my wedding day.

CHAPTER 3
DAY AFTER THE WEDDING
MELODY

I wake up groggily on Sunday morning. I flash back to the wedding and the reception that followed late into the night. I immediately head to the kitchen for much needed coffee! It sounds eerily quiet compared to the previous morning that was filled with chatter from the bridesmaids. I search the cabinets for something to go with my coffee and am thrilled to find some chocolate covered doughnuts left over from yesterday's breakfast. The morning is looking up thanks to chocolate!

While waiting for the coffee to brew, I sit at the kitchen table and replay last night over in my mind. It was so much fun to reconnect with some old friends from college. We email occasionally, but don't see each other as often as we would like. It brought back memories from such a happy time. I loved the scholarship house I lived in at FSU and we all became family to each other. I don't think I would have survived college without the support of those friends. There will always be a place in my heart for them and seeing them just brought back a flood of good feelings.

With the wedding behind me, I remember that I purposely left this day unplanned so I could devote some time to finding a song for *The Singing Melodies* for the big event. I pour a cup of coffee and take the doughnuts into the living room so I can get down to business. I spot an ink pen with hearts on it lying on the coffee table.

Hmmm, I haven't seen that before. One of the girls must have left it behind. I retrieve several song books from my piano bench and make myself comfortable on the couch. I pick up the pen in case I need to make notes while leafing through the pages of songs. I twirl it around in my hand to see the pretty hearts. Suddenly, some lyrics pop into my mind. "My heart has something to say" keeps playing in my mind. Maybe the hearts on that pen have triggered a memory, but I can't place the song. I concentrate as a tune forms with the lyrics. I can't place this song, but more lyrics spring into my mind. "So, listen, listen, listen," I think as I hum a tune. "As my heart whispers deep from within, listen, listen, listen." Words keep coming as I find some paper and begin writing them down. When one line is finished, another line forms in my thoughts. I write quickly for a few minutes until I discover that I have written an entire song. "Think!" I command to myself. "Have I heard this song somewhere before?" I know deep down that I haven't because none of it sounds familiar.

I carry my lyrics over to the piano and start playing a few keys, trying to match the tune that I'm hearing in my mind. It really starts coming together as I sing and play each line. I glance at the clock and am shocked to see that it's 3:00 already! I look back over my lyrics and tune and spend a few more minutes putting it all together in song form. Then, I sing and play apprehensively from beginning to end. And, I find myself totally moved as I sing the words. I start over and sing it with more emotion this time and realize that it is the perfect song for *The Singing Melodies*. It will showcase their talent and provide something original for the audience. I cannot wait to share it with the girls tomorrow! I hope they are as drawn to it as I am, or it will be back to square one.

I spend the rest of the day cleaning, then make a light dinner. After an hour or two in front of the television, I decide to call it a night.

I wake up Monday morning feeling a little nervous about sharing the song with the girls. I decide that I will sing it for them without mentioning where it is from. But first I need to get through my teaching day at college. Mondays are my favorite, though, as most of my classes are advanced and made up of students who are actually contemplating a career in music. The day goes quickly. As I am packing my briefcase after the last class, Chloe approaches me. She is probably my most talented student, and she seems to take her music more seriously than most of the others. We have discussed her future plans before, and I am aware that she has applied to attend The Juilliard School in NYC. I hope she is here to tell me good news about her application.

"Ms. Melody (she only calls me that when we're alone), can I talk to you for a few minutes?" she asks quietly.

I am in such a hurry to get over to the after-school program and see how my song is received, but I say "Sure, let's have a seat." I am preparing to listen attentively when tears start flowing out of Chloe's eyes. This catches me by surprise. She has always appeared happy and full of life. "What is it, Chloe?" I ask, while reaching for her hand.

"Ms. Melody, I'm in big trouble and I really don't have anyone to talk to about this. I'm sorry to be a burden to you."

I tell her that it's OK and to please continue. My mind flashes back to how serious everything seemed when I was a student.

"My parents are so proud of my music, and that I might even be considered to attend The Juilliard School. And, I've been hoping to get accepted." I think to myself that she must have gotten a rejection letter, when she blurts out "I'm pregnant!" I try not to let my face register the shock I feel, but I didn't see this coming. She continues, "I've had a boyfriend for over a year, but we were never intimate until about two months ago. His father died and he was so withdrawn. I couldn't stand to see him like that, and one thing just led to another. It was only the one time because I explained to him that I needed to put all my focus on my career right now. He was fine with it and we have actually grown much closer over the past two months. I started feeling bad and made all kind of excuses to myself when I missed my period. You can imagine my shock when I found out that I was pregnant. I've already been to a doctor to confirm it, but I haven't told anyone except my boyfriend. All I seem to be able to do is cry." And, with that last statement, she starts sobbing violently.

"Calm down," I say as I put my arms around her. "Sometimes things that seem horrible at first end up not being so bad. It's just the initial shock."

She cries even more and mumbles through her tears, "It's horrible. My parents will never understand. They expect so much of me and this is not how they raised me. They will be very disappointed."

I hug her again and say "Chloe, parents can be funny. You grow up thinking about them a certain way, and then they do something you would never expect. I am betting that your parents do everything they do out of love for you. They have always supported your endeavors, haven't they?"

She whispers a small "yes" through her tears.

"Well, this is just a minor change of direction," I say in my most comforting voice. "You may have to give it a little time to grow on them, but I think they will embrace you and whatever decision you make."

She quickly straightens up and says, "No, they must never know. If I get accepted to Juilliard, I can move there and not go back home for a visit until after I give birth. I should be able to attend classes up until the actual birth. The timing is right, and women do it all the time. I've already signed up with The Pregnancy Help Center and they will help me find a good family to adopt the baby."

I am so surprised by the tone in her voice that it takes me a minute before I can respond. "OK. It sounds like you have a plan, but I still suggest that you spend some time thinking about this before you finalize it. Everything is new and doesn't seem to fit into your plan currently, but plans can change. Please think long and hard about this decision. What did your boyfriend say?"

She dismisses his thoughts by saying, "He says he will do whatever I want. He is still trying to get through the loss of his father, and I don't think he can deal with this on top of it."

My heart goes out to her as I say, "I am always here if you need to talk." We hug again as she thanks me and forces a smile. I watch her as she leaves the room with her shoulders drooping and no bounce left in her step.

CHAPTER 4
DAY AFTER THE WEDDING
KATHRYN

I slowly open my eyes trying to figure out where I am and what time it is. The light is starting to seep in through a crack in the heavy curtains. I glance over to see my husband sleeping peacefully and remember that we are in a hotel room in Tallahassee. I lay still as I think back over the previous night. Lily looked stunning in her mother's wedding dress, and the ceremony was a dream come true for her. She had an inner glow that I have never seen before. I was doing okay until she started on her vows. Then my tears started flowing like a faucet! I tried to control them, but I think I got all the other bridesmaids started.

We made it through somehow and were relieved to move on to the reception. It was just like old times with all the family and friends we grew up alongside. We danced and ate, then danced some more. I don't even know what time we finally came back to the hotel.

As I lay quietly thinking about all the people that I saw last night, reality sets in and I suddenly remember that I have two weeks to put together an entire fashion show! I shake Rick to wake him up and then rush off to the shower. Within an hour the car is packed. We make a quick run through the lobby to grab some coffee and a bagel, the only interesting thing on the free continental breakfast that is so widely advertised. We refill our coffee to go and head back to Jacksonville.

My next few days are consumed with planning the fashion show. I mentally go through the list of possible models and start making phone calls. I pour over our new summer styles to decide which would make the most splash. As I am talking to each model, my mind is automatically choosing which dresses will best compliment her shape and coloring. I work non-stop through Thursday before realizing that while I'm making good progress on the fashion show, nothing else has been accomplished this week. I have been so busy looking through clothes and choosing accessories that I haven't been back to my office in days.

Deciding that it is time for a much-needed break, I head to my office to catch up on the last few days. As expected, slips of paper with messages are piled high. I pull a bottle of water and some yogurt out of my small refrigerator and begin the task of returning phone calls. Halfway through the stack I come across one from Melody. I remember that Lily is due to return from her honeymoon on Saturday. When we were planning the wedding, the bridesmaids decided to schedule a welcome home luncheon for the newlywed on Sunday. Melody probably called to be sure that I can be back in Tallahassee by the one o'clock luncheon. I think about the driving time, eating and visiting, and begin wishing that we hadn't planned it. Of course, back then I didn't have a fashion show to pull off single-handedly in a two-week period. The timing just could not be worse. I know it will be fun to hear about the honeymoon, but I'm tempted to bow out.

I dial Melody while silently going through my tasks and timeline for the fashion show. I am surprised when she answers. I respond, "Hi! It's Kathryn. I thought you'd be in class, so I was prepared to leave a message."

Melody laughs and says, "No, you caught me during planning period. Perfect timing! I'd like to run something by you, if you have a few minutes."

I tell her that this is the first time I've sat down in days. "I'm formally declaring it a lunch break, so talk away!"

Melody sounds apprehensive as she says, "I just want to throw out an idea. Please don't get excited or feel obligated in any way, as I'm not even positive this is a real opportunity."

That certainly piqued my interest, so I say, "Go on, you've got my attention."

Melody begins to explain about one of her students, Chloe, who confided in her that she was pregnant. "Chloe is an exceptional musician and has applied to study at Juilliard for the fall. She has worked long and hard toward this dream. The pregnancy is an unexpected result from one night of intimacy with her boyfriend, following the death of his father. She can't face her parents' disappointment, so she immediately signed up with The Pregnancy Help Center to give the baby up for adoption." She continues to fill me in on Chloe's plan to stay away at school for the last months of the pregnancy, in hopes that her parents will never find out.

"Wow." I murmur, "Poor young girl. But it sounds like she has her head on straight and knows what she wants."

Melody agrees, "Yes, she is a very strong young woman and works harder than any of my other students. Anyway, I thought I would mention it since I know you and Rick have started thinking about adoption. I have all the information on The Pregnancy Help Center. If you're interested, you might could call and explain how you heard about all of this and ask what the process is to apply."

I jump out of my chair and sing "Yes" into the phone. "Give me the information and I will call right away! Thank you, thank you, Melody!" I start writing down all the information.

Then, Melody says in her serious tone, "Please don't get your hopes up too high. As I stated, I'm not even sure there is a real opportunity. But I thought it might be worth a try. See what you can find out and we'll talk more at the luncheon, OK?"

"Great! See you then, and thanks again!" I hang up the phone feeling more hope than I've had in a long time. I dance a little jig and want to dial The Pregnancy Help Center's number right this moment. But I decide that I should talk it over with Rick first, even though I am sure of his answer.

I breeze through the rest of the day with renewed energy. I also plan how I will tell Rick tonight. There was no doubt that he would be on board. I have to work a little late, as I have been doing every day this week. So, I call Carrabba's (our favorite for Italian food) before I leave the office and order our favorite meal. I drive by to pick it up on the way home, and Rick is thrilled to see a good hot meal come through the door.

"Ummm" he says, as I set the table and unpack the food. "What's the occasion?" I fill him in on Melody's phone call while we enjoy our meal. I can tell that he is as excited as I am, but he is clearly the more logical person. "Let's take it slow," he says. "Would it be possible to meet Chloe in person? It would be helpful to talk to her and see what kind of person she is and see for ourselves if she is 100% sure of her decision. I don't want to take a chance on setting ourselves up for disappointment."

I think about Rick and how wise he is about decisions, and ask, "If I can get Melody to set up a meeting on Sunday after our girls' luncheon, would you be willing to ride back over to Tallahassee with me?" He is agreeable and immediately starts making plans to visit one of his friends during our luncheon. I call Melody, and within the hour she has an afternoon meeting set up with Chloe for Sunday.

"Chloe was happy to think that a friend of mine might end up raising her child." Melody says. "But she cried a lot on the phone and seemed unable to control her emotions. I just want to prepare you; in case she cries during our meeting." We talk a little about hormones and pregnancies and agree that we'll talk more on Sunday. I thank her and tell her how excited we are!

CHAPTER 5
DAY AFTER THE WEDDING
ELLA

I wake up Sunday morning with so many thoughts swimming in my head about the night before. This was my brother's wedding, so I am especially nervous about writing the article. I want to be sure to capture the spirit of the wedding, and to make my brother (and parents) proud. I decide to go to the eleven o'clock church service so I can spend a little time beforehand jotting down some notes. It proved hard to be a part of the wedding and take notes at the same time, so I am relying solely on my memory. I make a cup of hot tea and grab a breakfast bar as I head into my mom & dad's home office.

I decide to list anything that might merit mention in an article. I begin with the description of Lily and her dad walking down the aisle. I know it's a cliché, but she really was a beautiful bride. Her mother's dress was so delicate and feminine. And her bouquet of solid white lilies with purple irises added the perfect touch. Then, I try to describe the sweet look on my brother's face as he watches her coming towards him.

I have to mention the vows. I don't think there was a single dry eye in the house after Lily said her vows. They were so genuine and seemed to be spoken straight from her heart. I had never heard anything so heartwarming. I describe the bridesmaids' dresses that perfectly matched the purple irises in Lily's bouquet, then continue with descriptions of the food and drinks at the reception. I write notes about the dancing and the music that was provided by some of Melody's students from the FSU School of Music. They played everything from Stevie Wonder to the Rolling Stones – what talent! I list as many of the attendees as I can remember and describe some of the dresses that made an impression on me. I will use all these notes tomorrow at work when I get serious about the article. I just don't want to forget anything before then.

Later, after church service, I go back to my parents' house for a late lunch. My brothers usually join us on Sunday afternoons, but Travis bailed out since we were all together last night and Kyle is off on his honeymoon. I wonder if he will keep up this tradition now that he is married, and if Lily might join us. I can smell a roast the minute I walk in and my mouth starts watering. Luckily, Mom is ready for us to be seated at the table. We have plenty to talk about today as we re-live the wedding. This also helps me get a different viewpoint for the article. Since my parents know all our friends, we have lots of fun discussing them – what they wore and how they looked. Mom and Dad hadn't seen some of them since high school, so it is interesting to hear their opinions.

With my brothers missing, our conversation shifts more toward a focus on me. Mom and Dad seem really interested in my life and my goals, and we haven't had time to catch up since pre-wedding days. Now that Kyle is happily married, I guess they are going to delve into what's next for me. I dated a guy for about a year, but things didn't end up working out for us and there hasn't been anybody serious since then. I know they want me to find a partner in life, but there is nothing to talk about in that area, so I steer more to my career.

"How is your job going?" Mom asks. "Is it still as challenging as you thought it would be?"

I think about it for a moment before answering. "Yes, I love the day-to-day work of writing about all of the events in Tallahassee. It helps me to feel like a part of the community. I can be involved in most of the fundraising and community service events, and I mingle with the movers and shakers of our city. It's such a positive thing for me personally, as well as for my career. But I still have the big dream of writing a book someday. I've thought of several ideas, but none have really inspired me to get started. I guess I will know it if the right one ever hits!"

My dad agrees that it will happen when the time is right. "Ellabell (his nickname for me)" he says, "You'll be the next Harper Lee, just wait and see!" I smile and think to myself that it doesn't matter what I do in life, my dad will always be my biggest fan. He taught me that I can do anything I want to in life and that I should always follow my dream. That support has helped me through many classes and numerous interviews, being equipped with the confidence to believe in myself.

We talk a few more minutes about some of the family that attended the wedding. It provided a great reunion for us and was good to see some cousins that I hadn't seen in years. Mom talks about her sisters and how nice it was to catch up on everything. Most of them don't live very far away, but everybody is busy and it's hard to stay close. I glance at Dad and notice how tired he looks. "I think that wedding wore you out!" I joke.

He agrees, and says, "I see a nice long nap in my near future!" I laugh and hug him as he retires to the bedroom. Mom and I begin clearing dishes and chatting about Kyle and Lily's honeymoon.

"What are your plans for the afternoon?" Mom asks as we finish up the dishes.

"I'm going to start getting my notes together from the wedding. I won't actually write the article until after Lily gets back. I'd like to capture some of her thoughts. I also need to look over my schedule and prepare for next week. Thanks for that wonderful lunch and good conversation," I say, while heading toward my room to be alone with my thoughts.

CHAPTER 6
DAY AFTER THE WEDDING
LILY

I wake up early on Sunday morning to the shrill sound of an alarm. We didn't tell anyone that we were spending our honeymoon night in a local hotel. Now, we will spend today driving down to Miami to board the cruise ship for our honeymoon. Our ship is stopping at Cozumel and Grand Cayman Island.

We arrive at the dock and have fun boarding the cruise ship, waving to everyone as if we knew some of them. We check out our cabin which was even smaller than I was expecting. But we decide that it adds to the coziness of our honeymoon.

We immediately set off to tour the ship and check out all the activities. Never having been on a cruise before, I am stunned by how much there is to do onboard. Kyle and I go back to the room to unpack our suitcases, and then we head straight to the poolside bar to start relaxing! It is a gorgeous afternoon and we are tempted to stay in this one place, until we hear the announcement that the casino is open. After about an hour of Blackjack, we leave long enough to enjoy the buffet. It is Italian night and the aroma of the red sauce is sumptuous. The first thing anyone ever mentions about a cruise is the food, and it doesn't take long for me to see why. I try to commit this food to my memory for later stories about our honeymoon.

We retire early on this first night, exhausted by the

wedding and the drive down to Miami.

We head to the breakfast buffet early on Monday and it does not disappoint. We decide to spend the day lazing by the pool, then back to the casino for the evening. This full day of relaxing has helped us to catch our breath. The next morning, we are ready to go when the ship docks at Cozumel, Mexico. Cozumel is known for its crystal-clear blue water, so we spend the first half of the day snorkeling. I remembered to bring a disposable underwater camera and I wonder if the pictures will ever be able to capture the beauty of these fish... so many of them! We enjoy a late lunch at an outdoor café, and then walk the shops in search of souvenirs.

The rest of the week flies by too fast. The final night of the cruise, Kyle and I end the night at the Poolside Bar, which has become our favorite spot. I finally decide to tell Kyle about my mother's letter. I haven't shared this with him so far because I wanted a bit more time to cherish the thoughts of my mom and keep them safeguarded in my heart. Now, I decide that I am ready to share. I pull the letter out of my purse as we sip our drinks. I am once again taken over with emotion. I fight back tears as I tell him about the letter and hand it over to him. He reads it silently and gives me a warm smile as he hands it back.

"What a loving gesture," he says. "I noticed a calmness around you at our wedding and I wondered what had caused it. Now I know. What a lovely gift." I knew immediately that he understood what an affect this letter had on me.

"Yes," I say, "It made the day even more perfect than I could have ever imagined. I haven't known much about my mother since I was so young when she died, but this gave me a small insight into her life. It was an amazing gift and I think I will be forever changed because of it. I have not been able to get the thought of my mom sitting in the lily room out of my mind. I know the address of that house, and even drove by it once after hearing some of dad's stories from back then. If it's OK with you, I would like to research who owns the house now. Maybe they would let me walk through the house sometime. I haven't been able to stop thinking about mom's letter, and I would love to sit exactly where she was sitting when she wrote it. Would that be alright with you?" These were new feelings for me, and I wanted to include Kyle in on everything from this point on. I could tell from his face that he thought it was a very touching thing to do.

"Sure," he says, "I would like to go with you, if that would be OK." I knew right then that this man cared very deeply about me, and I thought about how lucky I was to find him. He warns me not to get too excited, though, just in case it all falls through. I agree that we will take it slow and see how it goes. We finish our drinks and make our way to the indoor lounge. A band is playing one of the songs from the Dirty Dancing movie that we love. Kyle offers me his hand and we make our way to one last slow dance. I allow myself to be swept away in Kyle's arms as I think back over our perfect week.

We wake up early Saturday morning and pack up our suitcases. The ship pulls into port at 11 a.m. and we find our car to start the long drive home. Kyle drives and we discuss our plans for next week. He is going back to work on Monday, but I have one more week off to get fully moved into his apartment. We stop for an early dinner and arrive home around 9 p.m. Saturday night.

We could only muster up enough energy to bring in the suitcases before collapsing on the bed.

We wake up early on Sunday morning and decide to enjoy a morning of leisure. It's tough to jump back into our world of responsibilities after a week of cruising. We sip our coffee and read the newspaper. I realize that we have not watched or read any news in a week. It doesn't take long to catch up, though, and it is still as depressing as ever.

I decide to call my dad to let him know that we're back, and to check on him. He answers and sounds happy to have us back safely at home. "How was the cruise?" he asks. So, I fill him in on some of our activities. Then I change the conversation.

"Thank you for the wedding, Dad. It was everything a girl dreams of, and more."

"Yes, and you were the most beautiful bride ever!" he says, sounding like a proud father.

"Thanks, Dad. I felt beautiful, so that's what counts!"

He pauses and seems to have something on his mind. "Did you open your mother's letter?" he finally asks.

"Yes!" I reply, "It was such a special gift, Dad. Thank you for saving it for me. Mom told me a little about your life together, and she wrote how much she loved me." I said as tears formed. "It was a powerful gesture that lived through all of these years, and it brought me happiness at the very moment for which it was meant."

"Oh good!" he answered. "She had some tough days there toward the end. I saw so much sadness in her eyes. But that all disappeared each time she laid eyes on you. You brought her such joy. I'm glad she was able to send you a glimpse of her love for you. Was that the only thing in the box?"

This jolts my memory. "No, actually there was also an ink pen covered with hearts. I don't think I put it back in the box." I say as I make a mental note to ask Melody about it. "It didn't look like an expensive pen, but maybe she was letting me know that she was writing from her heart. I sure didn't need the pen to know that, though."

Dad thought for a minute and said, "You know, I won a heart covered pen for her on our first Valentine's Day together. I knew that night that she was the one for me. Bring it with you next time and I can tell if it's the same pen."

I smile to myself, and say, "OK, that would certainly explain why she included it in the box. What a lovely thought." We talked a few more minutes before I remembered to ask, "Mom also wrote about the sunroom that she was sitting in while she wrote the letter. She said it was full of lilies! I would really like to see your old house and to sit in the same place where she was sitting. Do you know who owns that house now?"

He said that he didn't know. "A young couple bought it from me after your mom died. I knew that I couldn't stay there without her. But I think it has sold several times since then."

"That's OK. I plan to look up the tax records and find out who owns it. Maybe there is a chance that someone would let me see the sunroom."

Dad answered pensively, "Yes, but the sunroom may not even exist anymore. Someone could have changed or remodeled the whole house by now, Lily. Remember how long ago that was."

"I know, Dad, it's just a thought. I realize things may have changed, but it's worth a try." He agrees and offers to go with me if it all works out. "I would love that!" I say. "You could describe how everything looked back then." We talk a few minutes longer and I tell him that I will get back to him when I know something.

I start getting ready for lunch with the girls. Kyle is going to eat Sunday lunch at his parents' house, so we plan to meet back up later. I arrive at Applebee's and don't see any familiar faces, so I snag a cozy corner table in the bar area. Ella, Kathryn, and Melody come in within minutes of each other. "Let's order Bloody Marys!" Kathryn says a little too loudly. "I'm in the mood for a little spice." It doesn't take much to twist our arms, so we all order a Bloody Mary and something off the brunch menu. Applebee's is always lively on Sundays and we are all energized by the voices and laughter around us.

"So-o-o," Melody asks, "How was the honeymoon?"

I smile as I answer, "It was perfect and I'm none too happy that it's over. We ate too much, drank too much, and gambled too much – all the things people do on cruises. But we offset it by dancing, swimming, snorkeling, and even a couple of exercise classes. It was a perfect vacation!"

Kathryn says something about reality, but I was still thinking about our last night of paradise and didn't hear it.

"Look at her," Ella exclaims. "She's sitting there with that little smile on her face. I don't think we need to hear another word about the honeymoon – her expression says it all."

I feel a small blush appear as our laughter permeates the air. The waiter arrives with food, so that quiets us for a few minutes.

"It's true!" I say. "It was a perfect week. Not much else to say. So, let's move on to catching up. What's going on back here?"

As usual, Melody was the first to respond, "Well, I received bad news on Friday. My grant proposal was not chosen as one of the projects to be funded."

We all commiserated with her, and Ella says, "I can't believe it. Your music project fills such a void for those young girls. Do you know which projects were chosen?"

"No, they haven't published a list of winners. It was such a disappointment. Now I'm worried about the future of the music group. I don't think the school will have any extra money next year, so this may be one of the first things to go. I am scurrying around trying to think of another funding option but getting nowhere so far. If something doesn't give soon, their performance at Under the Stars may be their last."

"Oh no!" Ella replies. "Those poor girls will be devastated, won't they?"

Melody tries to sound more positive than she looks, "I will have to find a way to motivate them enough that they will continue practicing at each other's houses. It may work."

We all chime in, "We'll try to think of some other options!"

"Meanwhile," Ella asks, "How is practice going for Under the Stars? Did you choose a good song for them to sing?"

Melody's face lights up immediately. "Yes! I forgot that I haven't told you about that. I ended up writing a song. It sounded good in my head, but they breathed life into it with their voices. It's called 'Listen to Your Heart' and the girls have been practicing every day. I am not exaggerating when I say that it sounds like it was written just for their voices. I'm proud of the song, but much prouder of the girls."

"That is so impressive," Ella says, "I can't wait to hear it. Maybe I can write an article after the event that will spark some interest. There are numerous women's clubs that provide pockets of money for deserving groups."

This lifts Melody's spirits and gives her something new to focus on.

Ella continues, "Speaking of articles, Lily, can you come by my office one day this week? I've started the article about the wedding but would love your input."

"Yes, definitely!" I say. "Would Wednesday morning be good?" Ella agrees, and we both add it to our calendars. Then, I look up at Kathryn and ask, "How is the fashion show shaping up?"

She explains that it is moving along. "I started off worrying about being able to pull it together so quickly, but things are starting to fall right into place. With one more week to go, I have booked the models and have chosen most of the outfits. I'm working with Nordstrom's to work out the details. They just decided that I should take charge of the sound system and background music. So, that will be my focus this week. Then, just keep your fingers crossed that all of the participants show up and that an audience shows up to watch!"

Ella says "That is so exciting! I wish I could come over and cover it, but I don't think the Tallahassee newspaper would get excited about an event in Jacksonville."

Kathryn mentions that it's on a Saturday. "Is there a chance you could freelance it? Or, you might call the Jacksonville newspaper and see if they want someone to cover it."

Ella thinks about it and says, "Freelancing is a great

idea! I've never written an article that wasn't for the newspaper. Yes, this would be a great place to start!"

Kathryn claps excitedly over this! "Great, we'll touch base later. Thank you, Ella!"

On that positive note, I decide to confide in them about my mother's letter. "Instead of a B*Session today, I want to share something very dear to my heart with all of you." That silences the table as they all sit looking my way. "I was given an extraordinary gift for my wedding." I say, as their expressions asked for more. "My dad gave me a box that contained a letter written to me by my mother." Tears start forming as I continue, "She wanted him to give it to me for my wedding day." Everyone's eyes are welling up now as they break into smiles, so I continue through my tears. "She wrote it about a month before she died. She was sitting in their sunroom with me lying beside her." The others are going for tissues at this point and Kathryn passes one to me. "She told me about her and my dad's life as a couple, and she said that I completed their life together. She told me how much she loved me, and that she would be proudly beaming down at me as I walked down the aisle."

I had to take a break, so the others took their cue, "How wonderful!" "That makes me cry!"

Then Melody states, "No wonder you seemed to have even more glow as you walked down that aisle."

"Yes," I say, "I think it was the only possible thing that could've made my day even happier." I wasn't ready to say anything about looking into the possibility of seeing my parents' old house, since I wasn't sure it was even a real possibility. Everyone is smiling and there is not a dry eye at the table. I find myself wishing for someone to change the subject.

Kathryn saves me by saying, "I want to share something personal, too." All eyes moved to her now as she glances at Melody, and asks "Is it OK?" Melody nods, so Kathryn continues, "One of Melody's music students came to her with the news that she was pregnant. It was totally unexpected. The poor girl only slept with her boyfriend one time, in the heat of the moment after his dad died. Doesn't seem fair does it? As hard as I have tried and been unsuccessful, this poor girl gets it right the first time, but it's not the right time. Anyway, it could possibly work out to be a good thing. Rick drove over with me today and Melody is taking us to meet the young girl this afternoon. Her name is Chloe and she has already registered to put the baby up for adoption through the Pregnancy Help Center. It's too early to even be talking about this because so many things could go wrong at this point. We still have to meet and like each other, and I need to fill out forms, and send in a letter and go through the process. And, most importantly, the baby has to be born. Chloe is in the very early stages of pregnancy. "So, I'm trying not to get too excited!" she says jubilantly. "But, as you can see, that's not working too well."

Melody reiterates that there are still a lot of hurdles. I can tell she is worrying that this could end up being one more thing on Kathryn's list of disappointments. Ella and I both say that we will keep them all in our prayers, and I am truly feeling happy for Kathryn.

We finish our meal and give our good luck wishes to Kathryn as we leave. I think back over the lunch and realize how lucky I am to have these good friends.

CHAPTER 7
KATHRYN

I find Rick waiting for me outside of Applebee's. Melody texts Chloe and finds out that she is already waiting at the coffee shop, about a mile away. We drive straight over there and enter the brightly colored room. There is soft music playing and the room is filled with younger people, probably students. Most of them are on their computers or playing with their iPhones. I wonder if conversation is a thing of the past.

Melody has beaten us there and I spot her at a table across the room, sitting with a frightened looking young girl. Melody introduces us as we approach the table. I steal a glance at Chloe as we are getting seated. She appears so small and young that my heart goes right out to her. She wears her brown hair very short and stylish. It is a direct contrast to her big brown innocent eyes. She catches me looking at her and gives me a sweet smile, seeming to relax a bit. Melody takes our drink orders and goes up to the counter, leaving us three alone. Chloe surprises me by speaking first. "I'm glad to meet you, but I admit that I'm very embarrassed by my situation. If you had told me five years ago that I would be going through this, I would've told you there was no way. But, mistakes happen," she said softly.

It broke my heart. "Chloe, please know that we are not here to judge you. Melody gave us some of the background story. It sounds like this baby was conceived out of love, just a little too early. I think you are very brave to put the best interests of the baby first and foremost. I am sure many young girls would choose abortion as an easier and quicker way to solve the problem."

Chloe gasped, "Oh no! That has never entered my mind as an option. I am an only child and I've heard stories about how hard it was for my mom to get pregnant. They tried for five years. Once it finally happened, it was a real tough pregnancy. They call me their miracle child. So, I know firsthand how much a child can mean to a family. I understand that you've been trying hard for quite a while, too."

Melody returns with our drinks as I start filling Chloe in on our three years of trying to get pregnant naturally, then two tries at in vitro. Rick tells her that we have given up on everything and are solely focusing on adoption now. Chloe tells us more about her life growing up. She was the light of her parents' lives and we could tell that she had a happy childhood. I can see that she is blossoming into a very sensible young adult. We tell her about our lives, our work, and our dream of having children. "As long as I can remember, I've had a plan to stay home with our kids until they reached school age. I fell in love with Rick and he agreed with all my plans. I always thought we would have three or four babies right away. Deep down I know that I was born to be somebody's mother, but these past few years are making me question everything. It's hard to have that big dream in sight but never seem to get any closer to it.

Chloe shook her head in agreement. "I have always dreamed of being a musician and I've spent years working toward that dream. The timing of this baby could threaten everything I've worked toward. I couldn't raise a baby and pursue my dream. My parents would be so disappointed that they would quit helping me financially. My boyfriend, Kevin, is working hard toward his dream of being a computer programmer. I love him and I think that we will eventually marry, but many years down the line. She tells us more about her boyfriend and how devastated he had been by the sudden death of his father.

I could tell our time was coming to a close, so I decide to lay my cards on the table. "Chloe, we want this baby very much." I look into Rick's eyes and say, "And we would be such good parents." He shakes his head in agreement and I see the hope in his eyes. "But I want you to think long and hard about this. I don't want you to do something you might regret later."

Chloe shakes her head adamantly. "No, my decision is made. Kevin agrees and I can only hope that my parents never have to find out about it. I can see how badly you both want a baby and how hard you've tried. In listening to you, I can relate to my own parents' struggle for a child… for me. If you're sure, please write the letter to the Pregnancy Help Center. I've written down my name and the case number for you. Reference it in your letter and tell them your whole story. Tell them how we came to meet through your friend and my mentor." She smiles and mouths a 'Thank you' to Melody. "The way I understand it, they are required to accept as many letters as are submitted and turn them all over to me. But, ultimately, it is my decision." She smiles and says, "I choose you."

We jump up and hugs go around the table. I am sure our celebration draws looks from everyone around, but I do not care! We trade phone numbers and I tell Chloe that I will write the letter tomorrow. I don't even care that I have a fashion show! This is priority #1. I give

Melody an extra special hug and tell her that I will be in touch.

She opens her purse to look for her keys as we walk through the parking lot. "Oh!" she exclaims. "I forgot to ask Lily if she left this heart pen at my house. You didn't, did you?"

"No, but I love the hearts!"

Melody says that she found it on her coffee table the morning after our slumber party. "I was looking for a song for *The Singing Melodies* when I saw the pen. It seemed like the minute I picked it up, the words of the new song just jumped into my head. Isn't that funny?" Then she adds slyly, "What if it's a lucky pen?" And, she laughs at herself.

Willing to try anything, I grab the pen and say, "I am borrowing this! I'm going to think of it as lucky and use it to write my letter tomorrow. I may even sleep with it under my pillow tonight!"

Melody laughs. "You do that! But be sure to bring it back. I'll ask Lily and Ella about it. It might be their lucky pen and I wouldn't want it to get lost." We laugh and say our goodbyes. I drop the pen and Chloe's information into my purse for safe keeping.

The ride back to Jacksonville goes by quickly. Rick and I both are elated and filled with some of the hope that has been slowly draining away. We order Carrabba's carry-out when we are close to home (for the second time in two weeks!). I place it on our nice dishes while Rick pours wine and lights candles for the table. We needed this good news. Our struggles have been weighing us down, but now love was back in the air! We decide to retire to bed early, and plan to get started on the letter in the morning before work. We are trying to keep our excitement at bay – but we are failing miserably.

I quickly check the online website for the Pregnancy Help Center before heading to the bedroom. I want to find out if anything else is required along with the letter. There is also a form to complete, so I print it out and leave it on the dining room table. I find Chloe's information in my purse and spy the pen. I lay Chloe's information beside the form on the table and laugh to myself as I take the pen to the bedroom. Rick is in the bathroom, so I sneak the pen under my pillow. I am going for all the luck I can get! We finish getting ready for bed and then allow ourselves to talk about the possibilities. It is too late to contain our excitement. There is no turning back now. We kiss as we say our goodnights and Rick's hands slowly move down my back. It feels so good to be in his arms again. I know that our lovemaking has become strained because of the pressure that I'm feeling (and passing on to Rick). It is hard to act happy when your dreams are falling apart. I feel like a weight has been lifted today, and it has been replaced with joy filling my heart. I give myself totally to Rick and it feels so good. I let go of my worries and celebrate. I know that everything is going to work out. Chloe had said so… she chose us!

We both wake up early on Monday morning, still reveling in our hope. While Rick showers, I decide to start on the letter. I make some coffee, and then retrieve the heart pen from under my pillow. I still believe that it will bring the luck I need to write my letter. I begin by quickly filling out the form that I printed last night. Then, I turn my thoughts to the letter. After a few minutes of deep thought as I turn the pen over and over in my hands, my mind begins to fill and the pen glides across the paper. I capture my innermost thoughts about what loving parents we would be and how much it would mean to us to have a child. My writing can barely keep up with my mind. My eyes are moist, and I can feel a smile tugging at my lips.

Rick comes out dressed for work. He looks at me for a moment, and then says "Is it going well? You're smiling so I think that is a good sign."

I can't hide my optimism as I answer, "Please, can you take a few minutes to read over what I've written?" He reaches for the letter and sits down with all the calmness of someone who has absolutely nothing more important to do than read my letter. I love this about him! He reads silently for a few minutes as I nervously pour myself another cup of coffee. He finishes and looks up at me.

"This is perfect," he states. "You have managed to put all of our dreams of becoming parents into words." He hugs me as if we have already been chosen (which we have… Chloe said so!). Then, he kisses me and hurries off to work. I am on Cloud Nine as I get the completed form and letter ready to mail, then shower and dress for work. I am ready to face the week. Let's get this fashion show going!

CHAPTER 8
ELLA

We just finished our morning meeting at the newspaper office when I look up and see Lily heading toward my office. She is right on time for our meeting about the wedding article. "Good morning" I call out as I catch up and follow her into my office.

"Good morning" she replies. "Are you ready for me?"

"Yes, definitely!" We sit and I begin organizing my notes. I let her read over some of the things I've written, just to be sure that I remember them correctly. She suggests a few minor changes and fills in some blanks about a couple of the guests. It doesn't take long for us to have everything in order. After we wrap it up, I can't help but say, "Kyle told us that you were interested in seeing your Mom and Dad's old house. Have you looked into it any further?"

I can see the excitement in her eyes as she replies, "Yes! I found it in the tax records on-line. An older woman named Madeline owns it. I called and told her my story. She said that she would be happy for me to visit the house, but not to be too disappointed if things didn't look the same. We set up a time next Monday after work. Can you believe it was that easy?"

I can sense her excitement, so I add, "Remember what she said, though. Don't go expecting to see the sunroom looking exactly like your dad has described it and wanting to see it through your mother's eyes. Your

60

dad moved out of that house over twenty years ago. I am sure that every owner has made changes along the way."

Lily shook her head in agreement, "I know, I know. I am going without any expectations. It will just be such a treat to see the house. Of course, it will be a bonus if I can see exactly where my mother was sitting when she wrote my letter."

I try not to sound worried as I ask her if she is going alone.

"No, my dad and Kyle are both going with me. I think dad is interested in seeing what the old place looks like now. He will be able to describe how things looked back then. I hope it doesn't make him too sad. But I think enough time has passed and that he just wants to be there for me."

I change the subject by asking "Are you going to be able to make it to Jacksonville on Friday for Kathryn's big fashion show? I'm excited about covering something on my own – as an independent! Melody is going to ride over with me. You're welcome to join us."

Lily shakes her head no. "As a newlywed I don't feel like I should leave Kyle this early. He worked all week while I finished moving into the apartment, so we are looking forward to our first full weekend in it together. I hate to miss the fashion show, but Kathryn seemed to understand. She is so giddy lately with the prospect of Chloe's baby that it's hard to talk to her about anything else." We both agree and express hope that everything goes smooth with the adoption.

Lily gets ready to leave and says, "Good luck with the wedding article! When will it be in the paper?"

"It will run on Friday, so be sure to look for it. It's your five minutes of fame!"

"Thanks, Ella. Have a safe trip to Jacksonville and have fun covering the fashion show!"

CHAPTER 9
KATHRYN

At 5:30 on Friday afternoon I am feeling strangely calm about the fashion show that is scheduled to begin in an hour and a half. I am already at the Women's Club building. I realize what a coo it was that I was able to snag this place. It has been decorated beautifully by the members of the Women's Club. Lucky for me, they love to spotlight their clubhouse. I guess it helps them attract new members. I already have the runway laid out and am listening to the guys in charge of the sound system. They are conducting their final testing. All the clothes are in the back room and have been organized in proper order. Most of the models are arriving and heading to the backroom to get their instructions.

By 6:00 I have two women stationed at the front entrance to hand out programs, and attendees are beginning to trickle in. I see Ella and Melody enter, so I lead them to front row seats. Then I head to the back for final inspections. My phone vibrates as I'm walking. To my horror, it's Julia, one of my models. "Where are you?" I answer a little too loudly, while silently cursing myself for not checking on the models before now.

Julia explains that she has been in a car accident. "I am alright, but the police haven't even arrived, yet. Four cars were involved, and the traffic is crazy around here. I don't think I can possibly make it there on time. I'm so sorry!" she says through her tears.

I can tell how upset she is, so I try to calm her. "That's alright. We'll figure something out. You just need to calm down and take care of yourself. Don't worry about us." I sound much calmer than I feel as we hang up. I start racking my brain for a replacement. I peek out and see that the seats are filling quickly. As my eyes land on Melody and Ella in the front row, I realize that Ella is almost exactly the same size and build as Julia. She has never modeled but she is a very graceful person – and I am so desperate! She catches my eye and I motion for her to meet me at the door to the back room.

"Ella, I need you! One of my models has been in an accident and can't get here on time. Will you take her place?"

"What?" she says laughingly, until she sees the despair on my face.

"Please," I beg. "You are her size and all you have to do is walk slowly down the runway. Someone will hand you a dress each time you come back from modeling. Please, please!" I sense that Ella is a bit fearful and I can't say that I blame her. But she can tell that I'm not kidding.

"OK," she says. "But no guarantees about how I will look!" I shower her with hugs and lead her back to get changed into her first outfit. Then I ask the model who will be following her to go through any last-minute instructions with her. I wish them all good luck and give the emcee the cue to get started. The first four models run smoothly, doing just as they have been instructed. Then it is Ella's turn, and I am frozen as I wait to see what happens. Ella struts down the runway with a little more energy than the others. It is immediately noticeable that she lacks the typical swagger and has more of an athletic stride. She looks petrified until she reaches the end of the runway, then she flashes a huge grin. This is totally uncharacteristic of a model, but she suddenly appears to be enjoying herself. The audience immediately reacts with smiles and applause. I realize that I have been holding my breath, but it's going to be OK! The audience seems to love her freshness. She retreats and throws me a questioning look to see if she was passable. I give her the thumbs up signal, so she continues to prance. The rest of the show goes without any problems. Melody uses Ella's camera to capture some pictures of the models and the audience. At the end, the models all come out for a final bow. The audience gives an enthusiastic round of applause and all has ended well! I hurry back to thank the models and give Ella a special hug of appreciation, then rush out to mingle with the audience as they are leaving. I am thrilled that this is over, and I feel physically exhausted.

As everyone is clearing out, I see Melody and Ella leaving. "Thank you so much for coming!" I say as I hug them tightly. "Ella, I will never be able to repay you for that one. You were incredible!"

She gives a hearty laugh. "I don't know about that, but I sure did enjoy it… once I got over my case of nerves. I am really excited to write my article about it now that I have seen an insider's view."

I laugh with her, but something is nagging at me. There is something that I'm forgetting. Suddenly it comes to me! I reach into my small shoulder bag and pull out the heart pen. I hand it to Melody. "I'm returning this heart pen. I used it for good luck but want to get it back to you before I forget. Did you find out who owns it?"

Ella interrupts and says "Good luck? Can I use it to write my fashion show article first? I could use some good luck. I promise to return it."

Melody fills Ella in on the story of how she found the pen and wrote the song for *The Singing Melodies* with it. She decides that it must be Lily's pen if it's neither of ours, so she tells Ella that she can borrow it. "But, please be sure it gets back to Lily!"

I hug them both and thank them again as they leave. Then I struggle to help everyone clean, get the clothes organized, and loaded into the truck. We lock up the building and I make my way back home. Rick is waiting to hear about it, and I am excited to tell him. I sit on the couch while he goes to pour a glass of wine. The next thing I know, I wake up in my bed on Saturday morning. I feel like I have run a marathon and wonder if I am catching something, or if this has all been more stress than I realized.

Rick greets me with a cup of steaming coffee, "Good morning sleepy-head! You fell asleep before I even got the wine bottle open. But you did stay awake long enough to tell me that the show was a success." I tell him about Julia's accident and Ella filling in. I can tell that he is happy that it's over and hopes my stress will soon leave, too. We enjoy a nice lazy Saturday, which includes several naps on my part. It is just the kind of day I need.

CHAPTER 10
LILY

I wake up to the alarm clock on Monday morning. It will be my first day back to work since the wedding. I love my job but must admit that I have enjoyed my time off. I am going back to work as Mrs. Jamison today. It's a weird feeling to use my new name (when I remember to use it!). My day speeds by as I am busy trying to catch up on all that has happened in my absence. The day is over before I know it. I drive home to meet up with Kyle and Dad to go see the house. I can hardly contain my excitement! When I get home, Kyle and Dad are both already there. We chat for a few minutes, but hurry to get on our way. Our appointment is for 6:00, so we try to rush through the traffic. We pull up to the house right on time. We slowly make our way up the sidewalk while observing the outside of the house.

Dad starts by saying, "It's been so long since I've seen this place. But the outside doesn't look much different. Someone has kept it in good shape."

I'm too nervous to respond, so I ring the doorbell.

A small older woman opens the door and greets us with a warm smile. "Lily?' she asks.

"Yes! Thank you so much for inviting us into your home. This is my dad and my husband, Kyle."

"It is so nice to meet you all." she says. "My name is Madeline, but please call me Maddie. My husband and I bought this house about five years ago. He passed away shortly thereafter, so I have lived here alone for most of the time. I will lead you around the different rooms, if that's ok. Please feel free to ask questions, or whatever." She starts with the kitchen, which has been updated with new appliances and granite counters.

"Wow!" Dad exclaims. "This kitchen has come a long way. Lily's mother and I cooked many meals together in here, but it doesn't even look like the same kitchen."

Maddie answers, "The woman who sold it to us was the one who upgraded the kitchen. My husband and I had never seen such a nice kitchen, so it was a big plus for us." We slowly move into the living room.

Dad looks around. "This room actually looks about the same. Of course, the furniture is all different and the wood flooring has been added, but it still has the same feel." We follow Maddie through the bedrooms. Dad continues to point out the differences and similarities until we move out into the sunroom. We are all three speechless as we take in the beauty of this room. It is glass enclosed on all sides and is overflowing with roses – in every color!

"This is the most beautiful room I've ever seen," I blurt out. Dad is clearly moved as he looks around. Kyle is speechless and I know that he is trying to let us take it all in.

Dad says, "This room is spectacular. It was our favorite room when we lived here. We had rows of lilies on three sides and we would come in here to relax in the evenings. On weekend mornings we would bring our coffee in here and mull over the newspaper. The lilies were beautiful, and love always seemed to surround us in this room. I would have never believed it could look even more beautiful, but these roses are stunning!"

Maddie shows her pride as she says, "Thank you. I started planting them when we first bought the house.

Once my husband died, I spent many hours adding more roses and enjoying the solitude of this room. It saved me in many ways."

"This is amazing!" I exclaim. "You can feel the love in this room."

Maddie smiles, "I always could, but I didn't know anyone else could. Thank you. This room looked so sad when we moved in. It was mostly empty, but had a row or two of dead, dried up plants. The windows were filthy, and the air smelled so stale." She lets out a small gasp, and says, "Before I forget, I found a picture jammed into the far corner of the room. It was hard to see because of the old plants, but I noticed it when I started removing them. Let me go get it."

As she leaves, Dad starts describing the room as he remembers it.

She quickly returns and hands Dad the picture. "Do you recognize it?" she asks.

I see the recognition in Dad's face. "Yes, this is my wife, Sophie, and she is holding Lily. I remember taking this one day while we were all enjoying an afternoon... before she got sick."

I quickly move over to see the picture. My mother had her hair down and was facing the camera with a big smile. She was holding my face toward the camera and I looked so happy. We were sitting on a red wicker chair and there was a glass-topped end table beside the chair. The table had 4 metal legs that were shaped and painted to look like tall lilies. We were nestled among all the actual lilies in the background. I fight back my tears as I look into my mother's eyes. "She looks so happy." I manage to say.

"We both were." Dad says with a crack in his voice.

Kyle asks to see the picture, probably trying to give us a moment to recover. "Look at that beautiful table," he says. "It has lilies for legs. How unique!"

My dad looks as though he is smiling at a memory. "We found that at a little antique shop in St. Augustine. We were there celebrating our first anniversary and the fact that we had just found out that your mother was pregnant. She really loved lilies and went crazy over that table. We decided right then and there that if you were a girl, we would name you Lily."

"Thanks, Dad. That was a nice story."

Maddie exclaims "Oh! I still have that table. It's by my bed, so you couldn't see the legs when you looked in there. Come with me and I'll show you." We follow her into the bedroom and see it. It's a beautiful piece. Maddie explains that it was the only piece of furniture that she had bought from the previous owners. "They were trying to sell all of their furniture so they could start with a clean slate in their new house."

Dad tells us that the young couple that bought the house from him had wanted to purchase all the furniture along with it. "It didn't really seem like the type of furniture that would go in my new house, so I just left it all behind. I had far too many other things on my mind at the time. It was several months before I remembered that little table and wished that I had brought it to my new house. But it was too late to ask."

We go back to the sunroom and continue our conversation. Maddie asks about us and where we live.

"We're newlyweds!" I answer. "We have been married a little less than a month. We both had apartments, so we gave mine up and moved into Kyle's. It was bigger and closer to our jobs. It's also just across from the Tallahassee mall, so that's convenient."

Maddie is familiar with the area and agrees with its convenience. She tells us that she has recently hired someone to help her with the upkeep of her house. "I just can't get around like I used to could. You don't ever think about how difficult simple tasks can become as you get older. So, enjoy your youth while you can!" She laughs as she pats us on the back.

"We plan to do just that!" I say.

Kyle agrees and says, "We better get going. We've taken up enough of your time."

"Yes," I say. "Thank you so much for letting us into your home, and for the picture! You have given me a glimpse into a past that I really never knew much about. Now I can make my own memory out of it and keep it with me forever."

Maddie walks over and hugs me. "I get a little lonely here by myself sometimes, so please come back anytime." I dig a business card out of my purse to give her and tell her to call me if she ever needs anything.

CHAPTER 11
MELODY

As I sit at my desk, I am thinking how happy I am to only be teaching two classes during the summer session. Most students who take my class in the shorter summer session are those who just need a couple more credits, so they decide to take music as an elective. As I get about thirty minutes into the class, I am not surprised to notice a few students nodding. I hate summer session! I start thinking that we are all just wasting our time, but then I see a couple of bright faces that seem to be listening to my every word. So, I remind myself that if I only succeed in helping one student discover a passion for music, it will have been worth my time.

The day goes slowly, but I finally make it through both classes. I walk outside for a small break before writing up plans for tomorrow's classes. I glance up and am surprised to see Chloe coming towards me. She doesn't usually take summer classes. She sees me and starts walking faster.

"Chloe, I didn't expect to see you here today."

She is beaming as she announces, "I got my acceptance letter to Juilliard! I'm so excited! It's a dream come true!"

I do a little victory dance with her as I congratulate her. "Well done!" I say. "I guess you will be busy making plans for the fall – finding a place to live and all, huh?"

"Yes!" she says. "I have loads to do now that I can finally start planning."

I congratulate her again, and say, "You deserve it as hard as you have worked to get here. So, enjoy it and continue to work hard!"

She thanks me and turns to leave. "Gotta go! There's so much to do. I just wanted to share the good news with you."

I wave goodbye as she sprints off. I think to myself that it's odd that she did not bring up any other matters. But I chalk it up to the excitement of her acceptance news. And maybe she needs to relish the good news and forget her worries for a little while.

I finish my class plans, and then drive over to meet *The Singing Melodies*. School is out but they are letting us practice for our event in one of the smaller classrooms. I am a few minutes late and the girls are already lined up and ready to practice when I arrive. They start singing as soon as they see me, so I sit and listen as they sing the entire song. I break into applause and think about how proud I am of these girls. They go through it a couple more times before we sit to have our meeting. They already know that we did not get the grant and that we have no other source of funding, as of now. I don't want them to worry so I lay out my plan. "Under the Stars is the perfect time to kick off our funding drive. The audience will be made up of people from all walks of life. There will be women who belong to clubs that fund projects. There will be members of the community who are looking for ways to help support their community. You never know who will be listening. So, you girls just sing your hearts out! Then, I will follow up later with letters addressing our needs, while your performance is still fresh in their minds!" This seems to make everyone happy, so they reward me by practicing the song one more time. We plan our next practice date, and everyone is all smiles as we leave. I think about my plan as I am driving home. I know how hard it is to acquire funding, but I vow to try my best. At least I was able to sound confident around the girls. I want them to enjoy this experience with no worries, even if it does end up being the last thing we get to do.

CHAPTER 12
ELLA

I do not even notice the crazy Monday morning traffic as I drive to work. I am still exuberant about my real-life chance to model. It was such an awesome opportunity to participate in a fashion show that I was also covering. I think about how much I am looking forward to writing the article. I truly have an inside perspective that will lend much more to the story.

I spend Monday and Tuesday finalizing some articles at work, and I spend the evenings at home writing about the fashion show. While I am writing, I glance down at the heart pen in my hand and smile to myself. It may be just the luck I need (it couldn't hurt!).

I spend some time at work on Wednesday preparing for a book signing that I'm scheduled to cover later that evening. The author is from Miami and she is traveling around Florida to promote her newest book, entitled The Sunshine State of Mind. I read the book over the past weekend and thoroughly enjoyed it, so I am looking forward to the evening. I arrive early and there is already a line forming in the bookstore. I flash my tag and a young girl leads me back to the signing table. The author, Susan Faye, comes out right on time and immediately starts signing books. She is very friendly and tries to answer questions in the few minutes she spends with each fan. I stand off to the side and listen while taking a few pictures of her and of the crowd. She has her hair pulled back in a ponytail and is wearing a flowery sun dress that shows off her nicely tanned arms, looking every bit like you would imagine a girl from Florida should look. Susan takes a break after about 15 minutes of signing (as scheduled) and stands up to address her fans. She talks about her book and about her love for Florida. "I have lived here all of my life and I don't plan to ever live anywhere else. This book is a tribute to our state and all its beauty that I have grown to love and appreciate. Of course, there's also a little sex, murder, and mystery thrown in!" She laughs and adds, "I have to write what sells!" The fans adore her and applaud loudly. She thanks them for coming as she sits back down and continues signing while entertaining the crowd.

I find my mind wandering as I watch her. She is living my dream life. I want to write books and have fans – just like her. I wonder if there is a secret to her success. As I continue to watch, I realize how interesting she is, and I already know how talented she is as a writer. That's the secret! I now know the secret but that doesn't make it any easier. The other key ingredient has to be lots of hard work. I bring my mind back to the present and see that she is really working the crowd and appears to be enjoying every minute. I vow to myself to work harder toward this dream. The rest of the evening goes by quickly as I stay busy writing notes and taking pictures for my article.

The rest of the week is uneventful. I complete my article on the book signing and finish a few other small articles. Mom and Dad leave early on Saturday for a long day of shopping for treasures at the local flea market. So, I devote my entire day to finalizing my article on the fashion show. I read over the completed article with pride. I think to myself that this is my best work so far. Now, what am I going to do with it? I sit it aside for the time being, realizing how tired I am after a full day of writing. I decide to call it a day and head off to bed.

I wake up on Sunday feeling well rested after a good night's sleep. I shower and get ready for lunch with the family. Travis arrives first, with Kyle and Lily not far behind. I'm delighted to see that Lily has decided to join our family lunches on Sunday. It never hurts to have another female voice! Mom already has the food ready, so we choose our seats around the table. We all thank her and tell her how good everything looks.

Lily beams as she starts the conversation. She tells us all about their visit to her old house. I have noticed more happiness in her tone ever since the wedding. I wonder if it is due to married life, or if her mother's letter is actually the reason.

She is unusually animated as she describes the sunroom. "Maddie, the owner of the house, found an old picture of me and my mom. Here, let me show it to you!" she says as she grabs it from her purse. "Look at my mom and how beautiful she is. See how happy we look!"

They pass the picture around until it gets to me. I take one look and say "Wow, look how much you favor your mother!"

Everyone agrees, and Lily says "Dad and Aunt Cindy always said that I did, but this is the first time I have had a picture to actually see it. Thank you for saying it." Her face reflects how much this has meant to her. Everyone agrees with me and I think she is starting to get a little embarrassed by the compliments, so she changes the subject.

"Ella, I heard that you actually modeled at Kathryn's fashion show! What was that like?"

I was excited to tell her all about it. "It was such a treat. It was fun to wear the beautiful clothes and each outfit was perfectly accessorized. They did a much better job than I could ever do myself. But, on the flip side, I saw how much hard work goes into modeling. They make it look easy, but there is a lot going on behind the scenes."

Lily asks, "Have you started on the article, yet?"

I try to curb my enthusiasm as I answer. "I finished it yesterday! It was fun writing from the perspective of a spectator turned participant. It added so much more depth to the article. I am really proud of it. Now, I have to decide what to do with it – where to send it!" Lily suggests a few of the more popular women's magazines. I tell her that I am thinking about the Women's Monthly. She agrees, and I suddenly remember the pen. "Oh, and I wrote the entire article with this heart pen, just in case it's magic!" I say, as I retrieve the pen from my purse and hold it up.

Lily smiles and exclaims "That's mine! The pen was in the box with the letter from my mom. I'm not sure what you mean by magic. But now that I think back, I realize that I opened the box just before writing my wedding vows. I had been having trouble putting my thoughts into words. Then, I felt like my words all came together the minute I held the pen. I must have left the pen at Melody's house the morning of the wedding."

I squeal upon hearing this! I tell her what Melody had said about looking for songs for *The Singing Melodies* for their big event, when she noticed the pen lying on her coffee table. "She picked up the pen, wondering where it came from, and the words to a song started forming in her head. She used the pen to capture the words and ended up writing the new song for *The Singing Melodies*.

So, we started kidding about the pen being magical. And, now your story just adds to the magic! It can't hurt to believe. Besides, it's such a pretty pen."

"And it has a good love story." Lily adds. Then, she tells us all about her dad winning the pen for her mom on their first Valentine's Day together.

"What a great story!" I exclaim. "I may have to write about that one day!" We all laugh and finish the pot roast that my mom has served.

As we all prepare to leave, my dad comments on how much he has enjoyed the lunch. He thanks us all for coming. "It's nap time for me." he says and turns toward the bedroom.

Kyle mentions how tired dad looks, but mom says, "We are just getting old, son." We all voice our disagreements. Then, we say our goodbye's as everyone leaves to enjoy the rest of the day.

I help mom clean the kitchen and then adjourn to my room. I type a cover letter for my article and start packaging it up to mail to Women's Monthly magazine tomorrow.

CHAPTER 13
LILY

I hear the shrill of the alarm. Ugh – Monday morning! I go through the motions of getting ready for work without even thinking. I do remember to kiss Kyle on the way out. I shake myself awake for the Monday morning traffic. The first hour of work drags by while I work on a client's monthly ledgers. The phone rings and I jump as the shrill sound startles me. I answer "Hello. This is Lily Jamison." I surprise myself by remembering my new last name.

An older woman's voice says "Lily, is that you?"

I immediately recognize Maddie's voice. "Yes, is this Maddie?"

"Yes, Lily, I am so glad you answered. I wasn't sure if this number would ring directly to you, or not."

I am surprised to hear from her, so I ask, "Is everything alright, Maddie?"

"Yes, yes." She answers. "All is well. But I have been thinking about you ever since you visited. Something has been on my mind and I wondered if I could run an idea by you?"

I am relieved to hear that nothing is wrong. "Sure! I have also thought a lot about you and how nice you were to let us visit your home."

"Well," Maddie continues "I love my house, but lately I have worried that it is just too much for me to handle. It really is much more house than one person needs. But a house can become like part of your family… very hard to let go. I couldn't sell it to just anyone. But ever since I met you and your husband, I have felt like you belong in this house. And, I know you would love it as much as I do."

This catches me off guard, so I ask "Really? You would think about selling your house?"

"Yes," she answers. "But only to the right people. Have you and Kyle ever thought about buying a house and, if so, would you ever be interested in mine?"

"Yes, and yes!" I exclaim. "We discussed it at length before we married, and we even looked at a few open houses. But we didn't see any houses that hit us right, and we were too busy with wedding and honeymoon plans. So, we finally decided to put house hunting on the back burner and try again when we had more time. It is a big decision. But, as far as your house, I love it! If you are serious, I'll run the idea by Kyle. If he is open to it, I can call you back and schedule a time to get together and discuss your ideas."

"Wonderful!" she says. "I will finalize all of my thoughts and will be ready to discuss everything, just in case it all works out. Just let me know either way, OK?"

I tell her that I will call her back in the next day or so. "Thank you so much! We'll talk again soon." I hang up and immediately call Kyle's cell phone. I know he will be busy at work now but will check his messages at lunch. I leave a message telling him all about the phone call, so he can be mulling it over in his thoughts.

After work, I run through the grocery store and pick up a rotisserie chicken for dinner. I plan to cook some rice and beans to go with it, a quick and easy meal. This will allow us more time to have a long conversation before dinner.

"I get home before Kyle and I quickly change into

shorts. He arrives a few minutes later, so I pour two glasses of wine while he changes clothes. We make our way out to the small table and chairs on our balcony. I can't wait any longer, so I start with "What did you think about Maddie's phone call?"

He surprises me by answering, "It definitely interests me, if it does you. I thought the house was very charming and the location is great for us."

"I agree. I am definitely interested, too! I haven't been able to think about anything else. But I know it's too early to get excited. She didn't give me any idea of how much she might ask for the house."

"Right." he says. "And, we would need to go back and look at it more closely. You see everything in a different light when you think about owning it."

We talk a little more about our views on a fair price and what a great home it would be. I am delighted to realize that Kyle is totally on-board with me. We discuss our schedules for the next day and determine that we are both free the next evening. So, I call Maddie to ask if we can come by tomorrow after work.

"Yes," she says. "I have been busy thinking everything over, and I will be ready to discuss some specifics by then. Come right after work and we'll have drinks in the sunroom!" I hang up thinking that she really knows how to sell!

Tuesday goes by slowly as I struggle to concentrate on my work. Finally, the workday ends and I rush home to meet up with Kyle. When I discover that he has beaten me home, I know that he is as excited as I am. We discuss our budget on the drive over to Maddie's and agree that $250,000 is our max price. When we arrive, she already has white wine chilling in the sunroom. Kyle pours the wine while we all get comfortable.

Maddie starts by thanking us for coming. "Lily, I have done a lot of thinking since we spoke. When I started thinking about selling the house to you, I realized how happy the thought made me. So, I know that I am ready. This house is just too much for me. It's too much work and too much space."

I let out a sigh of relief! "But, what would you do?" I ask.

Maddie's eyes light up as she speaks. "I spent yesterday calling around to different retirement neighborhoods. There is a place called The Villages in central Florida. You can rent or buy a home, and the place offers so many activities and clubs. I can play bridge, join a sewing club, and work out in one of the sports pools. It has so many ways to stay active and to make new friends.

Kyle says "That sounds wonderful! This could be a win-win for all of us. Would you mind if we walked through the house again?"

"You certainly must," she says. "I'll just sit here while you take a closer look around. Then, I can answer any questions that might come up."

We take our time and walk slowly through every room. The kitchen and bathrooms have been updated and definitely reflect our taste. We note that the wood flooring is all new and every window has been upgraded. We agree that the house appears to be move-in ready.

"We wouldn't have to do a thing." I whisper to Kyle.

"You are right" he says, "But, that may cause it to be over our budget. It's a beautiful house."

"I agree! Let's go talk money and see if we're out of our league."

We walk back to the sunroom to join Maddie. Kyle asks a few questions about when the house was built and when some of the updates were made. I ask some questions about the neighborhood.

Then Kyle lays it on the line. "We love the house, Maddie. It is much more than any of the open houses we have seen. We are just not sure that we can afford it. We have been saving for our down payment, but we don't want to strap ourselves down with a huge house payment. Have you determined a price?"

Maddie answers "I think the house is easily worth $300,000." I can feel my shoulders fall and I know that Maddie can sense my reaction. "But," she continues, "My husband, Ron, and I were blessed throughout our careers and in our investments. And, we never lived a luxurious lifestyle. When Ron died, I realized that I had more than enough money to last my lifetime. We never had children, so I don't even have a grandchild to spoil. I would love to be able to help a young couple such as you. If you don't mind telling me how much you can afford, maybe we can work something out."

We glance at each other and Kyle says, "We agreed that $250,000 is the highest we can go and continue to live comfortably. We know that we can get approved for that amount, and we have enough for the down payment for that amount. I am sorry, but we promised ourselves that we would not get carried away and exceed our budget."

"Good for you!" she exclaims. "You must always live within your budget. I see a lot of Ron and myself in you two. So many young people go into debt these days to live beyond their means. I would be willing to sell the house to you for $250,000. I won't have to advertise it or hire a realtor, so that will be a savings for me. At this point in my life, it would make me feel good to help you get started. And, I hope you will love this house as much as I have. Please, feel free to think it over. It is a big decision and it needs to be the right one."

We look at each other and shake our heads. Then I say, "We definitely want it! I can't believe you would do that for us. Thank you so much. This is a dream come true for us!"

Maddie explains that she has a lawyer who would handle the closing for us, and that she would get a blank standard contract from him. We agree to meet again the next evening to complete the form and finalize our plans. "Would you be willing to wait 45 days before we close? That would give me plenty of time to find a house in The Villages."

Kyle answers, "That would be perfect! It would give me enough time to give written notice to our landlord. Maddie, we cannot thank you enough!"

I embrace Maddie tightly before we leave and tell her that we will be back tomorrow. We chatter non-stop on our ride home. Kyle and I both are elated about the house and agree that we need to do something nice in return for Maddie's kindness.

Kyle says "Maybe we can help her move. She doesn't have children and most of her friends are probably older, so she may need help. We can mention it to her tomorrow."

I call my dad the minute we get home. I figure that he will think we are rushing a bit too quick. I blurt out the whole story as soon as he answers. When he gets the chance, he says "Lily, that is wonderful! I know first-hand that the house has good bones, and it appeared to be totally updated. What a nice lady Maddie has turned out to be!"

I was so relieved. I really was not in the mood for bad thoughts or criticism. "Thanks for being as excited as we are, Dad! I couldn't wait to tell you. I'll call you again tomorrow and let you know if everything goes well with the contract signing." We hang up and Kyle and I spend the rest of the evening making new plans.

Time seems to crawl the following day at work. It finally ends, and we head back to Maddie's. She has everything ready for us to sign and has even invited her lawyer, Jim.

Jim explains that they are old friends. "Maddie does so much for me, so I always owe her a favor. Thanks for helping me get out of debt to her!" he laughs. We all sit down, and Jim explains how the closing process will work. Then he goes over the sales contract and answers all our questions.

We both feel totally at ease and ready to sign. I open my purse and retrieve the heart pen that I have remembered to bring. Kyle makes a comment about it, so I say, "It never hurts to have a little magic on our side!"

Jim and Maddie both have inquisitive expressions, so I tell them a shortened version of the story. They agree that we all need a little magic on our side, and we continue signing until all the pages are complete. When all the business is finalized, Maddie pours us a celebratory glass of wine.

Kyle takes the opportunity to ask her "Will you need help moving? We would be happy to help box things up, and even drive down and help you unpack."

She shakes her head, "No, I'm going to hire movers. I'm not up to tackling all of that. But, thank you for offering."

I say "Maddie, you have been so nice to us. We would like to do a little something in return. Is there anything at all that you need?"

She thinks about it, then says, "No, please don't feel like you owe me anything. Having you move in this house is making me very happy. I know how much you will love the place. You are getting to move back into the first house you ever lived in – the house where your parents lived when they had you. I love that story and I love being part of that story. It does my heart good!" We finish our wine, say our goodbyes, and agree to update each other on any progress.

The rest of the work week and the following week fly by. We stay busy making timelines for all the tasks we need to complete, such as notifying our landlord, transferring some of our services, and cancelling some of the other services. We are totally consumed between work and making moving plans. So, when Friday arrives, we are excited to be going out. The Under the Stars event is tonight and most of our friends will be there. Plus, it's Melody's night to shine with her girls, and we will be there to support her.

CHAPTER 14
MELODY

I wake up early and think "It is finally Friday!" I worry that this may be the girls' biggest and last appearance. Everything is so up in the air that it starts to dampen my spirit. "No," I tell myself. "You are going to put those thoughts out of your mind and enjoy the moment!"

I suddenly remember that I will have to go on stage to introduce *The Singing Melodies* tonight, and I am glad that I splurged on a gorgeous new dress. The dress is tan with a turquoise and brown paisley print on it. It is very slimming, and it just happened to match a pair of tan heels that I already had. I love it when that happens!

I am thankful that I have summer classes to keep my mind occupied today, and I jump up to get started on my day. The morning passes quickly. I spend the afternoon getting a manicure and pedicure. I finish my appointments, then head home to relax for a few minutes before dressing for the big night. I plop down in my oversized chair and feel my muscles relaxing. Then, I remember that I didn't turn my cell phone back on after my appointments. I dig it out of my purse and notice a message from Kathryn. I know that she is probably on her way from Jacksonville and wants to touch base or wish me luck. I listen as she says "Melody, I am on my way over. I'm so excited about tonight. I just wanted to tell you good luck, in case I miss seeing you before the performance. Tell the girls to break a leg! Isn't that what they say in showbiz? Also, don't forget that we're meeting for breakfast tomorrow. I know you have a lot on your plate, so I'm just reminding you. See you tonight!"

Realizing that I'm much too excited to relax, I put my CD of Nikki Sue into the player. She has always been one of my favorites. I start getting ready while her voice permeates the room. I need to arrive early anyway, so that I can meet up with the girls in *The Singing Melodies*. They will be so nervous. I am glad that we are going on first, and then I can relax and enjoy Nikki Sue's performance. As I finish getting ready, I steal a glance in the mirror. I love the new dress and feel so good in it! This boosts my confidence and I am ready to tackle the evening!

I arrive early and the place looks magnificent. The large ballroom has been transformed to look like an outdoor theater. Trees have been placed around and lights are strung across the ceiling to look like stars. Round tables that seat eight fill the floor. I heard that the event was sold out, which means we can expect about 300 people. *The Singing Melodies* arrive in two groups of three girls each, accompanied by two of the mothers. I bought matching red shirts for them a couple of weeks ago as a reward for their hard work, and they all paired them with black pants. They look great, and I cannot believe the effect that this has had on them. They are standing straighter and exuding more confidence than I have ever witnessed from them. They are chattering non-stop and their voices reflect their excitement. We are led to a table up front since we are part of the entertainment. A hostess informs us that we should go to the backstage area in about twenty minutes.

"Let's sit for a while and watch everyone come in." says one of the girls.

This fits into my efforts to keep them all together, so I agree, "Good idea! Does anyone want a glass of water or anything before we sit?" They all decline and are clearly more interested in people-watching. They ask if we will get to see Nikki Sue backstage. "I don't know. She may be one of those stars that arrives just in time to take the stage… who knows? I would like to see her, too!"

People start slowly drifting in, getting their drinks, and mingling with each other. Before long, there is a steady line coming in and the sound of so many conversations is almost deafening. I notice the time and announce, "Girls, it's time to go backstage. Is everybody ready?" They all shake their heads and jump up to form a huddle behind me. We quickly make our way to a backstage that is humming with activity. Several people look up as a lady makes her way over to us.

"Welcome! I am Rita and I will be giving you your cues tonight – where to stand, when to go on stage, etc. For now, please stand in this area to the left of the stage. I will go out first and welcome the audience and thank them all for supporting the hospital by attending this event. I will point out some things in their programs, and then I will introduce your group. Follow me over here to the left so we can see the stage." We move to the left and huddle around her as she continues. "See the tape mark out there on the stage floor? That is the center of the stage, so try to center your group around that mark. You will sing your song, then remain a minute or two for the applause before exiting on the opposite side of the stage. The walkway leads out to a side door, and you can walk quietly back to your table before the next group takes the stage. It should be fairly easy. Any questions?"

I raise my eyebrows up to the girls. They just giggle while they shake their heads "No."

"Thank you, Rita! I'm Melody, the music teacher that sponsors these girls. We are very excited to be here. I was told that I could say a few words about the group. Is that correct?"

Rita answers apologetically, "Yes, I am sorry! I totally forgot that part. Once you get situated in place on the stage, please feel free to step up to the microphone and say a few words."

"Thank you! I would like to introduce the girls individually since there are only six, and briefly tell how the group was formed. Is that OK?"

Rita shakes her head up and down while saying "Please remember to be brief and that will be fine. I will be going on stage in about fifteen minutes. Now, I need to go over and speak to the Boys Choir that will be following your performance."

The girls bubble over with excitement and nervousness for the next five minutes until one of them sees Nikki Sue enter the backstage. Suddenly, they all freeze and don't utter a sound. I am aware of how little time we have, so I quickly walk over to her and introduce myself and tell her how much I love her music. She thanks me with a warm smile, so I boldly continue. "I am a music teacher and those girls over there are *The Singing Melodies*. They go on first tonight and you would make their night if you could spare a moment to come meet them. They are some of your biggest fans. We all are!"

"Of course, I'm nothing without my fans." Nikki Sue says as she follows me over to the group. "Hey Girls! It's nice to meet you all and I love that name – *The Singing Melodies*. What will you be singing tonight?"

The girls took turns answering. "We're singing a new song that our teacher, Ms. Melody, wrote."

"It's called Listen to your Heart."

"And, we named our group after Ms. Melody!"

Nikki Sue smiles and says, "Very cool! I'm looking forward to hearing it. I will be listening from backstage. Nice to meet you all and good luck on the song."

The girls go crazy after she walks away. It is all I can do to keep their voices down until Rita walks back over to stand with us.

"It's show time!" she says, as she calmly walks out onto the stage.

The audience gets so quiet that you could hear a pin drop. Rita delivers her speech just as she had described to us, and then I hear her introduce *The Singing Melodies*. We bounce out onto the stage and the two middle girls do a good job of standing on each side of the center mark. Two more girls line up on each side of the center girls. They look toward the audience and their faces are glowing from the lights. I walk up to the microphone, trying to keep my trembling to a minimum. As I introduce each one, they smile and give a small wave. I continue with a quick summary of how the group formed and what a difference it has made in the lives of the girls. Then, as an afterthought, I give a quick laugh and say, "We are always looking for sponsors, if anyone is interested!" Then, I move to the side and watch the girls give a flawless performance. The song was perfect for their voices and they sang with such emotion. I have never felt prouder than I did at that finishing moment. The audience erupts with applause. The girls break into huge grins and take turns stepping forward to give a small bow. They turn and walk single file as they follow me off the stage. I give each one a quick hug as they step off the stage. Then, we quickly exit through the side door and make our way to our table as Rita comes out and introduces the Boys Choir.

The rest of the night plays out like a dream. Nikki Sue sings her heart out and the audience is mesmerized. Her talent is spellbinding. We reward her at the end with a standing ovation.

I ensure that all the girls get back to the proper place, and then head for home. What an exhausting night – but such a success! I undress and head straight to bed. With Nikki Sue's voice playing in my head, I quickly drift off to sleep.

I wake up feeling totally rested on Saturday. I'm looking forward to meeting the girls for a quick breakfast since Kathryn wants to get back to Jacksonville. I arrive and spot Kathryn, Lily and Ella already seated at a corner table. I see them clapping as I make my way over.

"Here comes the star of last night!" Ella cheers. The others join in with their congratulations.

"Did you all have as much fun as I did?" I ask.

"YES!" they all say in unison. And, they take turns telling me how much they enjoyed listening to the girls.

"Melody, the song you wrote was beautiful." Lily says. "And, so were the girls' voices!"

"I was so proud of them." I answer. "And, what about Nikki Sue? What an entertainer!"

We all agree that the night was more fun than we'd had in a long time. After talking about the performances and the people for a while longer, I finally ask "So, what's new with everybody?"

Lily says, "I've got news! Kyle and I are buying a house – and not just any house. We are buying the house that my Mom and Dad lived in when I was born."

"What?" says Kathryn. "How did that happen?"

Lily fills us in on her idea to go see the house. After getting the letter from her mother, she wanted to see the exact spot where her mother had written it. We all listen in amazement as she tells us about meeting Maddie and how everything just fell into place.

"Congratulations!" I say as she finishes. "What a wonderful turn of events. Lily, I'm so happy for you."

"Thank you! And, there's more. Maddie had found a picture buried in the plants when she moved into the house. It was of Mom holding me. Let me show you." She digs out the photo and passes it around.

"Your mom is beautiful." Kathryn says. "You look just like her!"

"She looks so happy." I add. "And, look how cute you are!"

Lily tells us a little more about it and that they plan to close on August 8th. "So, you are all invited over on August 11th. Mark it on your calendar."

We all pull out our phones excitedly and mark our calendars while continuing to congratulate her.

"I'll bring a huge Taco Salad to eat." Ella says. "We wouldn't want to mess up your kitchen so soon." We all shake our heads in agreement.

"Kathryn, how is everything going with you?" I ask.

"Wonderful! We haven't heard any news about Chloe's baby yet, so we are still trying to contain our excitement. But, it's too late for that. We are on Cloud Nine and have been busy with ideas for the nursery. We don't plan to actually make any changes until we get the final word, but we will be ready as soon as the phone rings!"

We all cheer for her and click our coffee cups together. It is so good to see her happy again.

"How about you, Ella? How's it going?" I ask.

"Everything is good in my little corner. I finished my article on the fashion show and submitted it to Women's Monthly Magazine. It turned out well and I'm going to give it my best shot at getting published. If this magazine doesn't want it, there are plenty more to try. It's time for me to start working on my career, and I'm not taking no for an answer."

"You go girl!" I say. "Don't slow down until you get to the top. I can't wait to read it."

"Way to go, Ella!" Lily says. "Good luck and keep us posted. I love hearing all these happy stories. We are all in such good places, and all at the same time. I think this is a first!"

"Right! No B*Session today." says Kathryn. "Let's end on this happy note. I am heading back to Jacksonville and need to get on the road. I may not be back until we meet at Lily's new house on the 11th. So, everybody keep up the good work."

I add, "Don't forget that I am going on a two-week cruise in a couple of weeks. Some of us professors are going to squeeze in some last-minute fun before the new school year starts. I'll tell you all about it on the 11th."

"Yeah, rub it in." Ella says, as we all head to our cars.

I spend the rest of the day relaxing and planning for the cruise. Packing two weeks of clothes requires a lot of planning. I go to bed thinking about my friends and all the good things I heard today. I don't think I can remember a time that we were all in such a happy place at the same time. I can feel my smile as I slowly drift off to sleep.

CHAPTER 15
ELLA

I wake up early on Sunday and decide to go to the first church service. Kyle, Lily and Travis are coming over for a late lunch, and I want to get home in time to help Mom with the cooking. As I walk into the kitchen to see if anyone turned on the coffee, I hear Mom scream my name from her bedroom. I run to the bedroom to see her cradling Dad on the bed.

"Call an ambulance!" she shouts. "Something is wrong! He is not moving!"

I grab the phone and dial 911 as fast as I can. My mind is racing as someone answers and tells me that an ambulance is on the way. I try to calm Mom while checking Dad's pulse. I can hear an ambulance already approaching. I run to the door and usher the paramedics to Dad's room. Mom and I hug each other as they begin working on Dad. They ask Mom a few questions while they are trying to revive Dad. They work furiously as Mom and I hold onto each other, shaking and crying. All at once, they all stop, and the world seems to be at a standstill.

"I'm sorry." One of the men says quietly. "He's gone. Nothing else can be done. He appears to have had a heart attack and we were not able to save him. I'm so sorry…" his voice trails off.

Mom screams and runs over to Dad. I go over to hug her and try to calm her as the men leave the room. We cry and hug Dad and say a few words to him. My head finally clears, and I walk out into the living room where the paramedics are waiting. They ask some questions about which funeral home we would like to use, and I realize that I have no idea. Mom must have overheard because she slowly comes out of the bedroom, looking so much older than the night before. We sit while she answers questions, and the ambulance finally leaves with my dad's body.

"Mom, why don't you lay down for a little while? I'll call Kyle and Travis. I'm sure they will come right over."

"Ok. I won't sleep, but I would like to be alone for a few minutes." she whispers, as she moves toward the bedroom.

I make the calls and Travis arrives within minutes. We talk quietly until Kyle and Lily arrive. Mom appears soon after and we all spend the day together. We discuss funeral plans and make the necessary calls to other family and friends. After they leave, I realize what a blessing it is that I am living at home. Hopefully, I can help Mom through all of this. I tell myself that everything happens for a reason, but this doesn't stop me from crying myself to sleep.

We schedule the funeral for Thursday. I decide to take the week off from work and help Mom with everything that needs to be done. Kyle and Travis also take a few days off. Monday and Tuesday pass by in a fog. Both of Dad's brothers arrive on Wednesday, along with a couple of cousins. Melody and Lily are at our house as much as they can be, helping with visitors, food, etc. Kathryn calls every evening to check on us. Mom tries to keep herself busy by looking after everyone else.

Finally, the day of the funeral comes. Afterwards, our house is overflowing with family and friends. We trade stories about Dad. Some are funny and some are sad.

There are some that I have heard over and over through the years, some that I lived through, and some new ones that I can't believe I have never heard. Through them all one thing is clear, Dad was loved by many. I am at the top of that list, and I wonder deep down how much this will change my life. All I know with certainty is that it will.

The out-of-town relatives all leave on Friday. Kyle, Lily, and Travis spend most of Saturday and Sunday at the house with me and Mom. Mom proves to be a pretty strong woman as we all discuss the changes in her life. By the end of the weekend, I am sensing that she will be alright as she makes this journey through a new chapter in her life.

CHAPTER 16
MELODY

My first thought when I awaken is about how nice it is to have a couple of days to relax and prepare for the cruise. I will drive down to Tampa on Wednesday morning in time to board the ship that afternoon. I am looking forward to vacationing with some of my fellow professors and getting to know them a little better.

My thoughts quickly switch to Ella and her family. Last week was tough on all of them. I know that reality will set in this week. Ella is supposed to go back to work today, so I make a note to call and check in with her this evening.

I decide to get up and start the day off right by cooking myself a good breakfast. My plan is to stay home and pack all day. The phone rings while I am pulling eggs and bacon out of the refrigerator. I don't recognize the number, so I answer with my professional "Hello, this is Melody."

"Hi, Melody. We haven't actually met, but I saw you at the Under the Stars event a little over a week ago. My name is Margo Sherman and I am Nikki Sue's manager."

"Oh... yes. Wasn't that a fun night?" I ask while trying to hide my shock at getting a call from Nikki Sue's manager.

"Yes, it was a fun night. And, your girls were certainly a highlight. I will get right to the point if you don't mind. Nikki Sue loved the song that the girls sang. She remembered one of the girls saying that you wrote the song. Is that correct?"

"Yes, thank you. I wrote it about a month before the event, with the girls in mind. I am so glad that Nikki Sue liked it."

"In fact, she liked it so much that she wanted me to ask you if she could possibly record it. Nikki Sue said that your words evoked so much emotion, and she thinks that her voice could convey that same emotion.

"Really?" I ask in disbelief. "Oh, my goodness… of course. It would be an honor to have Nikki Sue record my song. Wow… I'm floored!" I can hear my own rambling, so I force myself to stop.

"Great! I could come to Tallahassee tomorrow, if you have any time available to meet."

"Yes, I am off work for the summer break. So, it's a perfect day to meet. You name the time."

We finish the discussion by planning to meet at 10 a.m. at a coffee shop near my house. We agree that it will be a quiet place to talk. I hang up and shout "Whoo-hoo!" to my empty house and dance a jig as I prepare breakfast. I sit down to eat with so many questions popping into my head. Will they pay me for the song? Do I need a lawyer, or a contract? This is so far out of my league that I decide to meet with Margo before I do anything – or tell anyone. I am floating on a cloud the rest of the day as I try to concentrate on everything I will need for the cruise. At the end of the day, I sit and enjoy a nice glass of wine and allow my mind to imagine hearing Nikki Sue singing the words of my song on the radio.

After a fitful night of trying to sleep while my mind is racing, I get up and prepare for the meeting. I grab a pad of note paper and list any questions that come to mind.

I really don't know what to expect, so I just list all my thoughts.

I walk into the coffee shop a little before 10:00 wondering how I am going to recognize this lady. Then I see someone waving me over. She is very attractive, and I am surprised that she looks a few years younger than me.

She stands up and says "Hi. I'm Margo. I recognize you from Under the Stars. Thank you for taking the time to meet with me."

"Sure, I have been pretty excited since your phone call. But I admit that I have no idea what to expect, so I am probably not prepared."

"I figured as much. Not many people would know what to expect, so don't worry. Let's grab a cup of coffee and just talk."

We get our coffee and return to the table. Margo starts by asking all about the song. "Is it totally your creation? No one else owns any part of it?"

"Yes, I wrote it while I was alone at my house on a Sunday afternoon."

Margo explains that Nikki Sue would like to purchase the sole rights to record the song, but that the song would always remain mine as far as the writing credits. She walks me through the legalities and the recording process. "Nikki Sue usually writes her own songs. So, she has never done this before. As you know, a song may or may not ever make the charts – so there are no guarantees. For this reason, Nikki Sue would like to offer you a percentage of the profits of the song instead of a fixed dollar amount. She also was quite taken by your group of girls and the way you mentor them. The whole idea got her started thinking. She would love to do something like that herself one day, but she knows that it is not possible at this time with her schedule and travel. She wondered if you would be open to partnering with her on a special type of endeavor. Her initial thoughts were that you and she would collaborate on setting up a non-profit organization for the sole purpose of sponsoring young girls' singing clubs… much like your group. You and Nikki Sue could work together to hire the right people to oversee the organization. And, of course, your group of girls would be the first one sponsored. Nikki Sue realizes how lucky she is to be in her position. She would like to give other girls the same opportunities that she has been given. She would donate some money to get the organization started, then would like to propose the following split for the profits of your song. You would get 50% and the remaining 50% would go to the non-profit organization. Your 50% would be payment for the song as well as pay for helping with the non-profit. What are your thoughts about this type of project?"

"Are you kidding?! I can't believe my ears. This is perfect, and I love that Nikki Sue thought of it. Yes, count me in!"

"I had a feeling that you would react that way. I hope you don't mind that I did a little on-line searching into your background last week. Nikki Sue is a very caring person, and I can tell that you are as well. I think this partnership will be very successful. Now, we just need the song to be a hit! If you agree to the percentage split, I will go back and get all of the papers drawn up."

"Yes!" I say, as I pump my arms up in victory.

Margo continues to explain the process of signing the papers, creating the corporation, and recording the song.

"I'm leaving tomorrow for a two-week cruise. Will

that be a problem? Is there anything I need to do immediately? I will be back on August 8th."

"No problem. I'll have the papers drawn up and sent to you on the 8th. You can read through them, take them to a lawyer… whatever you need to do. At that point we will schedule a meeting between you and Nikki Sue to finalize everything."

"Perfect! Please tell Nikki Sue how excited I am about all of this and how thankful I am for the opportunity." We firm up our plan and I drive back home with my head spinning. I decide not to share any of this until things become more final. I am well aware that ideas don't work out exactly as planned sometimes, and I don't want to jump the gun. Once home, I get back to my packing. My mind keeps wandering back to Nikki Sue and my song. The phone interrupts my thoughts and jars me back to reality. I grab it and give a quick "Hello. This is Melody."

I hear mumbling and it sounds like crying. I finally recognize that it is Chloe. "Chloe, is that you? What's wrong sweetie?"

"Ms. Melody, I need to tell you something and I have just been dreading it." She says between sobs. "I can't give up my baby. I am so sorry! But the more I thought about it, the more I realized that I already love this baby – whether the timing is right, or not. I finally told my mom and dad last night, and I was shocked by their immediate support of me and any decision that I make. They reacted with such love and said they totally understood how things don't happen as we plan them sometimes."

"Chloe, that's a good thing. I am happy to hear it. So, calm down. I can handle the situation with Rick and Kathryn. Have you talked to your boyfriend?"

"Yes, Andy is thrilled." she says as her sobbing slows. "He agreed with me that the more he thought about it, the more he wanted to keep the baby. We plan to get married in a quiet ceremony next week. He plans to move to New York with me until I finish at Juilliard. Can you believe it?"

"Congratulations, Chloe. I am thrilled to hear that you are still planning to attend Juilliard. Don't give up on your dream. You may have to work a little harder, but I know you can do it!" I try to sound as confident as I can.

"I know it will be hard. But Mom has offered to come to New York to help in the beginning. Andy works with computers and hopes to be able to work out of home most of the time. I think we'll be able to coordinate our hours. I'm really looking forward to it, Ms. Melody. I'm just so sorry to have filled your friend full of hope. And, now I'm taking it all way. I can't bear to face her."

"You don't have to face her. I'll take care of it for you. This is not the end. Rick and Kathryn will have other chances. I'm glad to see things working out for you, and they will be too. Have you called the Pregnancy Help Center, yet?"

"No, I wanted to be sure that Kathryn found out from one of us first and not from them. I owe her that much."

"Good thought. I'll call her today, so you can call the Pregnancy Center tomorrow."

"Thank you, Ms. Melody. I'm grateful to you for everything you've done for me. I will never forget it." She says through more tears.

"You just continue working hard on your career and family, Chloe. That is all the thanks I need!" I hang up and drop my head. I cannot believe that I have to call Kathryn with this news. She and Rick will be devastated. I can't help but cry as I think about it. I finally pull myself together and decide to postpone the call until this evening. I wouldn't want to upset Kathryn at work.

I spend the afternoon finishing up my packing. This news has dampened my mood, and I am dreading making the phone call. Deciding that I have put it off long enough, I finally prepare myself and dial the phone. It rings three times before Kathryn picks it up.

"Hi! It's Melody. Is this a bad time to talk?" I ask, while secretly hoping that she will say yes.

"No, we are just finishing up our dinner. There is never a bad time to talk to you."

"Well, you may not say that when I'm finished. I have got some bad news to share, so I am just going to say it. Chloe has decided to keep the baby." I am heartbroken at my own words. I hear Kathryn gasp, and then repeat my words to Rick. "I am so sorry Kathryn. I feel like this is entirely my fault for ever getting you involved."

"No, Melody. It's not anybody's fault. I am actually happy for Chloe, and I hope it turns out to be the right decision for her." She sniffs and says tearfully, "We are disappointed. But I know in my heart that there will be another chance. It will happen when it is supposed to happen, and I truly believe that."

"Thanks for letting me off the hook, Kathryn, but my heart goes out to you both. I agree that it will happen when the time is right. And, I sure hope it is soon!"

"Me, too! Who knows? The Pregnancy Help Center may already have another baby that needs some parents. I'll call them tomorrow and see what the process is for our application now."

"Good! Stay positive. I'm leaving for my cruise

tomorrow, so I will be out of pocket for the next two weeks. I get back on the 8th and I will see you at Lily's new house on the 11th, correct?"

"Yes, have a great time! Please don't worry about this. Enjoy your cruise! I will want to hear all about it on the 11th. Bon voyage!" she says with all of the cheer she can muster.

I hang up and cry quietly for a few minutes. Life seems so unfair at times. But I do believe that things happen for a reason. Sometimes we just can't imagine what that reason might be. I think back over my day. It has been filled with emotional highs and lows, all in a matter of hours. I decide to clear my mind – no more dreaming of chart popping songs or worrying about babies. I pour a nice glass of Chardonnay and turn my thoughts to the cruise.

CHAPTER 17
KATHRYN

I hang up the phone after hearing from Melody that Chloe has decided to keep her baby. To say that I am devastated would be putting it mildly. I turn to Rick and see the sadness in his eyes. We hold each other for a long time while I cry, and I can tell that he is crying too. We finally let each other loose and try to finish our meal.

"Hon, this is just a small delay." Rick says. "I know there is a baby somewhere who needs us as much as we want him. I feel sure of it."

"I know you're right. But it doesn't stop my disappointment. I let myself get too excited over this one, so the fall is harder." I start clearing the table and realize how exhausted I feel. The news has hit me hard. "I am going to bed. I feel beat." I say, trying not to sound as dejected as I feel.

"Alright, honey. I'll be in there in a little while. Sleep it off because tomorrow we are going to wake up and put this behind us. We will only look forward because I know it is going to happen."

"I agree." I say as I kiss him on the cheek, then head for the bedroom.

I wake up Wednesday morning to the smell of bacon frying. Rick is already up and making us breakfast. What a nice thought. I get up slowly, and immediately feel nauseous and dizzy at the same time. I make it to the doorway to see Rick before everything goes blank.

The next thing I know, Rick is cradling me, and I hear my name.

"Kathryn! Kathryn, honey, are you OK?" he says loudly.

"Upset stomach…" I manage to say. "Maybe I worked myself into a tizzy…sorry!" I manage to get up and make it to the bathroom before everything comes up. "Ugh." I mumble. "I'm going to have to miss work today."

"Definitely. I'll call the doctor and schedule an appointment, just to check you out. Stress can affect our bodies in many ways and the doctor might help."

"I don't think I need a doctor. It just feels like an ordinary bug or virus. But I don't feel up to arguing about it either, so go ahead and call." I say, as I crawl back into bed.

Rick wakes me up around ten o'clock to tell me that he has scheduled an appointment for eleven. He tells me that he stayed home from work so he could take me.

"Thank you. Let me take a quick shower and I'll be ready in a few." I try to sound better than I feel.

"Can you eat a little something? How about a piece of toast?" he asks.

"I'll give it a try after I dress." The shower feels great and makes me feel like a human again. I dress, and then choke down a piece of toast and a cold Coke. I am starting to feel better and really want to cancel the doctor appointment. But maybe he can give me something to take the edge off my stress. That wouldn't be a bad thing.

Rick stays in the waiting room while Dr. Jones asks me questions and runs more tests than I could possibly imagine. He leaves the room for a few minutes so that I can get dressed, and then returns with Rick. My first thought is that this must be bad if he felt the need to bring in Rick. I can see the worried look on Rick's face, too.

Dr. Jones asks us to have a seat. Then, with a huge grin on his face, he announces "Kathryn, you're not sick… you're pregnant!"

"What? Are you sure?" That is all I can manage to say.

"100% sure! You appear to be about six weeks along."

I cannot believe my ears, but I decide to trust the doctor. I grab Rick and hug him, then hug Dr. Jones as if he has personally given me this gift. He knows how hard our journey has been so he hugs me right back and says, "May I be the first to congratulate you!"

When we get home, Rick treats me as if I am going to break. He is so sweet. "You know you can't keep this kind of treatment up for the next seven and a half months, so you better not even start it." I say laughing.

We spend the rest of our day off in absolute awe of the way things have turned out. We laugh and cry and make plans. We discuss whether we will find out the sex of the baby and decide that we are not ready to make that decision. We make a pact to keep this news to ourselves for a couple of weeks. We want to relish the good news alone and don't want to jinx it in any way. I start counting back the days to calculate when this could have happened. Rick and I were not intimate much back then due to the stress of the failed in vitro (and everything else!). Six weeks ago, was the week after Lily's wedding. I remember the lunch at Applebee's on the day after Lily returned from her honeymoon, and meeting Chloe later that day. We were elated about Chloe's baby, and we made beautiful love that night for the first time in so long. That had to be it! We relaxed and enjoyed each other… and it happened! And, I had the heart pen under my pillow! Melody said the pen might be lucky. I'm a believer!

"Rick, do you remember the night we shared after meeting Chloe in Tallahassee?"

"Yes, I have already thought back and that is the only night it could have been. We were not exactly enjoying much time together back then."

"That was such a wonderful night, though. Our baby was definitely made with love."

CHAPTER 18
ELLA

It is crazy here at work on Monday after being off all last week. It helps to take my mind off how much I miss my Dad. It has been hard on Mom, although she is trying to put on a good show. I am looking over my schedule for the week when I hear my cell phone ring. I decide to answer it since most people know not to call me at work. I try to sound cheery when I answer but know that I am not successful.

"Could I speak with Ella Jamison please?" a woman's voice asks.

"This is Ella."

"Hi! My name is Sherry and I am with Women's Monthly Magazine. I am calling regarding the fashion show article you submitted to our magazine."

"Oh, yes, it's good to hear from you."

"We really enjoyed your article. You gave it a unique perspective by writing as a model and as a journalist. It sounded as though you were writing straight from your heart, and it certainly gives a different appreciation of the fashion show. We would like to run it in our upcoming September issue. We are devoting over half of the issue to fashion and your article fits in very nicely. It appears that we have never used one of your articles, so I will need to email a contract to you that explains our payment and other legal issues. If it all sounds good, just sign the cover page and fax it back. But I do need it as soon as possible."

"That sounds wonderful!" You can email it to the address that I included on the submission. I will read it immediately and fax it back."

"Excellent. And please feel free to make future submissions. Once we have run one of your articles, it usually makes it easier to publish more in the future."

"Thank you! I look forward to it. I'll be watching for the email."

"Very good. I will send it right over. Thank you."

As happy as this news makes me, I feel the tears welling up in my eyes. I bury my face in my hands and let the tears flow. My dad has only been gone a little over a week. He always believed in me and taught me to work hard for anything I wanted. This is my first real success and, hopefully, there will be many more. My dad is the first person I would want to call. I am crying for all the things that I will never be able to share with him.

My desk phone rings and reminds me that I am at work. I grab a tissue, blow my nose, and then try to answer with as much professionalism as I can muster. It is my boss wanting to discuss a new assignment. Another author is coming to town for a book signing and she wants me to cover it, so I ask questions and make notes. The call helps to calm me and gets me back into work mode. The author is unknown to me, so I spend the next hour researching her work. It turns out that she is a children's author, and from the sound of her books, this should be a fun assignment. I decide to take a break and peek into my email. My inbox contains a letter from Women's Monthly. It is refreshing to have someone follow through on their word. I pull it up and read through it. I am pleasantly surprised to see that the payment for my article is more than I expected. All the legal verbiage seems straight forward. I print the cover page, sign it, and fax it back immediately. Then, I get back to work in order to stop my mind from getting too carried away over my small success. But I find that I am holding my head higher and beaming with pride as I work through the afternoon.

CHAPTER 19
THREE WEEKS LATER
LILY

We wake up on our first Saturday morning in the new house. Maddie quickly found her perfect house in The Villages, so we were able to close a few days earlier than expected. She left the house spotless. She also surprised us by leaving a housewarming gift – my mom's table with the lily legs! It will now be my night table, and there will always be a lily on it. We have worked ferociously for the past few days to get things somewhat organized, and it is beginning to take shape. We jump up to make coffee, and then go straight to the rose room... the most beautiful room I have ever seen. One side is filled with a round table and 4 wicker chairs, while the other side is occupied by two chaise lounges with a small side table in between. We sit down at the table and enjoy our coffee, as well as the peace and quiet of the morning.

"I cannot imagine there is a more peaceful place anywhere in this world." I say, as I sip my coffee.

Kyle agrees. "It is the perfect place to start the day and end the day."

"I never would have believed that we could own a place like this, Kyle. I feel like this is where we belong."

"That is weird" he replies. "I feel the same way. This is the place where we are meant to build our home and our life together. And, I don't think I have ever seen you this happy."

"Exactly! I feel a sense of contentment like I have never experienced before. Maybe it's loving you. Maybe it's knowing my mother's love. I think it is everything coming together at the right time, like nothing I have ever imagined. Kyle, I am even thinking about a family for the first time in my life. Us... with children. Does that scare you?"

"NO!" he exclaims enthusiastically. "I've been thinking the same thing. But you always said that you would never have children, so I keep trying to put it out of my mind. I am so glad to hear you say it!"

The rest of the day passes in a dreamlike fog. I think about what a happy turn my life has taken. I devote my attention to preparing for the girls' visit. We have not seen each other in a while. I am so excited to catch up, and to show off the new house. Ella volunteered to bring taco salad, so there is not much to do for the lunch. I set the table in the rose room and place a chilled bottle of white wine in an ice bucket. The doorbell rings and I see all three girls have arrived at the same time. "It is so good to see you," I say with all my heart. They look just as happy to be here as I am to see them.

"This is beautiful!" Kathryn says. "Give us the royal tour."

I hug them all, and then start leading them around the rooms. Ella places her salad on the kitchen counter as we pass through. They all ask questions and compliment everything along the way.

"I am so jealous!" Ella says. "All of this room!"

Our last stop is the rose room and gasps are heard all around.

"This is breathtaking" says Melody.

"Beautiful!" Kathryn chimes in. "I didn't think this room could be any prettier than the lily room in your picture. But it is even lovelier."

"Thank you. And, I agree. Have a seat and pour some wine. I'll go grab Ella's salad!" Upon returning, I glance at my friends as they are talking and laughing and think about how much these friends mean to me. We pass the salad around and talk about how long it's been since we were all together.

"We brought housewarming gifts. Open mine first!" says Ella. I unwrap the gift to find a framed picture of me and Kyle at the wedding. The article that Ella published in the newspaper is centered below it.

"Oh, I love this!" I exclaim. "Thank you so much! I have just the perfect place to hang it in our bedroom."

Melody hands me a wrapped box next. I open it to find four exquisite wine glasses with hand painted roses on them. "Beautiful! I should have opened these earlier and we could be drinking out of them. But, no worries. I will have many more opportunities to put them to good use. Thank you!"

Kathryn hands me a big bag stuffed with tissue. I gingerly pull something out. I realize that it is an antique shadow box in the shape of a heart. "Oh, it is so beautiful!" I exclaim. The others agree and try to get a closer look.

"I found it at an antique shop in Jacksonville and it called out to me," she laughs. "So, I had to buy it. Now you have to find something to put in it."

"That shouldn't be too hard. I'll give it some thought. Thank you all. You didn't have to bring gifts. But I sure do love them! And, it is so good to be together again. Let's hear some good news! Who is first?" I ask.

Kathryn looks sheepish, and declares, "I cannot wait a minute longer!" We all look her way as she smiles the biggest smile I have ever seen. "I am pregnant!"

I am sure that our screams were heard by neighbors! Kyle came running in to ask what was wrong. He got caught up in our celebration, and then quietly excused himself after adding his congratulations.

"Wow!" I say. "I certainly was not expecting that one!" The others agree, and Kathryn fills us in on some of the details of how and when they found out. Kathryn also tells us that Chloe had already decided to keep her baby, so everything had ended well!

Melody then says, "Well, that is hard to beat, but I do have some news too. This is crazy exciting for me, and it all happened so fast. The day before I left on the cruise, Nikki Sue's manager called and came to Tallahassee to meet with me. Long story short... Nikki Sue is going to record my song!"

"Wha-a-at?!" we all scream again. Kyle tries to ignore us this time. I think the last time was too much excitement for him. He peers in quietly and motions that he is going to the store. He is visibly relieved when I nod and give a little wave.

"And, that's not all," Melody continues. Then she tells us about the non-profit and their plan to fund young girls.

"I can't believe that." I say. "That is like your dream coming true."

She fills us in on some of the particulars. We ask her questions about the timing and tell her how unreal it all seems.

Then, I realize that we have put Ella in a tough spot. She has had so much sadness with the death of her father and I don't even know what to say, when she surprises me by saying, "This is not quite as exciting as either of those, but I am getting my fashion show article published in Women's Monthly magazine. And, I'm getting paid for it!"

We shower her with hugs and screams. When we finally calm down, Kathryn asks, "Well, Lily, how about you? Is married life and owning a new home all that you thought it would be?"

"Yes, I feel like I'm living my dream, and it's a dream that I didn't even know I had. All of my feelings… love, happiness, contentment have taken over my life."

"I can definitely see a change in you," notes Kathryn. And, the others agree.

"I honestly think it all started with my mother's letter. It's as if she sent all of her love into my life. Not that I didn't have love before, but I have always felt like something was missing. Her love opened my eyes to all of the other love surrounding me. Right after I read her letter, I picked up the heart pen and wrote my wedding vows in minutes. I had been agonizing over finding the right words, and it was like she sent them… from her heart and right through the hearts on the pen. And I know how funny that sounds, but I truly believe it!"

"Yes," Ella says. "I've been thinking about that, too. After you wrote your vows, you left the pen at Melody's house. And, what happened, Melody?"

"I was searching for a song for *The Singing Melodies*. I picked up the pen, and suddenly lyrics began forming in my mind. I wrote the entire song with the pen… as if it came straight from my heart!"

"Right," Ella continues. "And, I borrowed the pen to write my fashion show article. The lady from Women's Monthly even said that the article sounded like it came straight out of my heart. I have thought about all of this and whether it could possibly be tied together. But Kathryn, you took the pen to write your letter for Chloe's baby. Then Chloe changed her mind. That would've broken the chain of our hearts being fulfilled through the pen and the love of Lily's mother."

"But," says Kathryn. "You had mentioned that it might be a lucky pen. So, the night before I wrote that letter, I slipped the pen under my pillow. I felt the love and I believed that it was going to answer my prayers. Rick and I were so full of happiness that night after meeting with Chloe. Well, one thing led to another and it was the most romantic night we had shared in months. We have counted backwards, and I am positive that it was the night that we got pregnant."

"Yes!" shouts Ella. "Lily, your mother's love came through you and to all of us. I think it is a miracle."

"Ella," I say as my mind races ahead. "You have to write about this. This is the book that you have been waiting to write! And Kathryn, I know just what to put in my shadow box… my mother's letter and the heart pen."

Ella decides to give serious thought to writing our story. She tells us that she might be calling to get our thoughts if she ever gets that far.

Melody entertains us with some funny stories about her cruise. "One thing is for sure," she says. "I will not be traveling with co-workers ever again. You have to be on your best behavior… and that's no fun!"

We all join the laughter. The time flies by quickly and it is soon time for them to leave. We end the luncheon with big hugs all around. We are not sure when we will see each other again, so we agree to keep in touch by phone.

After the girls leave, I wander out to the porch to

enjoy the beautiful day and wait for Kyle to return. I arrange our two outdoor chairs and a side table on the front porch, then plop down in one. I notice a girl on the porch of the house across the street. She waves and starts walking across the street toward me. She carries herself as if she has the weight of the world on her shoulders. But, as she gets closer, I can see that she appears to be close to me in age.

"Hi. I'm Julie. Welcome to our neighborhood." she says with a guarded smile.

"Thank you! I'm Lily. We're thrilled to be here. How long have you lived here?"

"My husband and I moved here about three years ago. It's a nice, quiet neighborhood."

"Please, sit down for a little while if you have time. I'm just waiting for my husband to return from the store. I had some girlfriends over, so he made a break for it the first chance he could."

"Ok, I'll sit for a few minutes. Where did you move from?"

"My husband and I are newlyweds and we had moved into his apartment. But I actually lived in this house when I was born. I guess you knew Maddie?" I ask.

"Yes, I knew her well enough to speak when we saw each other. I never really thought we would have much in common, so I didn't push it any further than that. So, have you always wanted to move back to this house?"

"No, we moved when I was only one year old, so I didn't actually have any memories of the house." I begin to tell her pieces of the story about my mother dying, and that Dad and I had moved closer to relatives. And, since everything is so fresh in my mind, I continue with the story of my mother's letter and how it brought me back to the house. Poor girl! She probably didn't bargain on having to listen to my whole life story. But she sure was doing a good job of trying to appear interested.

"Your story has such a good ending. Unfortunately, they don't all end that well. My mother walked out on our family when I was a teenager. She fell in love with another man. He didn't want children. So, she left me and my younger brother with dad, and never looked back. Dad was so angry that we never even spoke of her. He did the best he could to raise us, but he was busy with work. He tried to have a social life too, which left even less time for us. We managed to make it through, but it wasn't easy. None of us are very close, and all three of us would probably rather forget that time in our lives."

"That is so sad. Have you ever tried to get in contact with your mother?"

"No! Why should I? She obviously didn't want us in her life. And, now the feeling is mutual. I became such a loner after she left that I honestly thought I was destined to be alone. But then I met Robert. He is an only child and somehow things just clicked with us. Now I'm not so alone."

"No kids?" I ask.

"Never! No kids, no close friends… just he and I against the world. I can't believe that I have opened up to you. It has been a long time since I talked to anyone about anything serious. Thanks for listening."

Kyle pulls into the driveway about that time. I introduce him to Julie and she quickly excuses herself to do some task that needs to be done.

We go inside and I show Kyle the gifts from my friends. He helps me secure the pen and my Mom's letter in the shadow box. Then, he helps me hang the shadow box and the framed wedding picture from Ella.

We have a perfect spot for them both since our furnishings are still pretty scarce.

We pour ourselves a glass of wine in our new hand painted rose glasses and move into the rose room. I catch him up on all the events of the afternoon, starting with my friends and ending with our neighbor. I declare that my first gathering in our new house was a total success and we toast to many more.

The next morning Kyle decides to tackle the front yard. Maddie used a lawn service, so it is in good shape. Kyle mows while I continue unpacking boxes in the house. As he finishes, I bring out two glasses of cold lemonade and we sit comfortably on the porch.

A few minutes later, I see Julie making her way over with someone who I assume is her husband. She introduces Dave to us, then Kyle goes to the garage to retrieve two more chairs. We all chat easily, and I think about how wonderful it is to have these new neighbors. Julie is more reserved, even a little sad, but Dave makes up for it with his non-stop talking and laughing. We ask lots of questions about the neighborhood and learn a little about our other neighbors. They stay for about an hour, then leave to make a grocery run.

I hear my phone ringing and make a mad dash inside. It is Ella and she is obviously excited as she is talking very quickly. I hear her saying "I have decided to write our book! The book about your mother's love and the magic of the heart pen! I've been thinking on it all week and already have my chapters completely outlined."

"Oh Ella, I am so excited! You are just the person to write about our magical story... since you lived it with us. Oh! You need to come get the pen before you actually start writing it!"

"I definitely will!" she continues. "My next step is to start filling in the chapters while it is all fresh in my mind. The pen will inspire me, and I could use some magic! I have only run into one major problem. I cannot seem to end it. We have all realized some of our biggest dreams, and we fully believe that the pen and your mother's love helped us all. But, how can I end it? Do I just write that we all live happily ever after? That seems pretty lame!"

"Hmmm" I say as I think on it for a minute. "I'm not sure. That's a good question for all four of us. Let's take some time to come up with the right thing." Ella agrees and says that she will call Melody and Kathryn to get them thinking.

The next week passes by quickly. We take our time unpacking the remaining boxes and organizing the contents. We run into the neighbors a few times and always stop to chat. Friday afternoon arrives and Kyle and I are so happy to relax in the rose room as we catch up on each other's week. We are looking forward to a weekend of enjoying our house when an idea comes to me. "Kyle, would you like to invite Dave and Julie over for dinner tomorrow?"

"Yes, that's a great idea. I'll get the grill set up and I can cook steaks." The idea of our first dinner party invigorates us both, so I call Julie and they sound just as excited.

We spend the next day getting the house ready and shopping for the meal. Julie and Dave walk over, and we serve drinks in the rose room. They admire the surroundings as we fall into easy conversation. I ask Julie if she would like a tour of the place.

She answers with a resounding "Yes!" I give her the grand tour that ends up in our bedroom. She admires our new wedding picture and article that Ella framed.

"Wow, that is really nice!" she says as she turns. Then her eyes lock on the heart shadow box with the pen and letter. "Is this your mother's letter?" she gasps.

I fill her in on the story of the pen being included with the letter from my mother. I smile as I tell her that my friends and I believe that the pen is magical. "That's all I can tell you. And, we have good reason to believe!"

We enjoy a wonderful meal. Kyle's steaks were grilled to perfection. He is such a master griller! The guys sit outside while Julie and I move to the kitchen to get things washed and put away. Our conversation drifts back to Julie's mother. I can see that this relationship is something that she regrets, even if she doesn't admit it. I ask again if she might think about contacting her mother.

She starts slowly "The thought has come up over the years. I've always figured that it would result in more rejection for me. So, I never gave it a chance. But it has been in the back of my mind ever since our first conversation. Your mom's letter seemed to add so much happiness to your life, but my circumstances are completely different. It could open up old wounds that have been closed for years."

"Yes, that's one ending. But it could also open the door to beginning a new relationship with your mother. She may want it even more than you. At least give her a chance."

Julie dries the last of the dishes, and quietly says "I am going to do it. I am going home and write the letter tonight before I can talk myself out of it again. I think I am finally ready to face whatever happens."

I smile and tell her to hold that thought for just a minute. I turn and run to my bedroom, open the shadow box, and gently remove the pen. When I return, Julie is looking perplexed as I give her a warm hug. "Please, use my mother's heart pen to write the letter. I am convinced of the love that flows out of it."

Julie's eyes begin to tear as she quietly whispers, "Thank you."

The next morning Kyle and I are surprised by how late we sleep. Maybe all this moving and entertaining has worn us out!

"I think I will try to squeeze in a nice run before lunch at your mom's." I announce. "It's a beautiful morning and I have been neglecting my exercise."

I finish my four miles feeling exhilarated as I sit on the porch to cool off. A minute later, Julie comes out and heads my way.

"I did it!" she shouts as she gets closer. "I wrote the letter to my mom! I sat down with a piece of paper, held the heart pen, and just started writing down all of my thoughts. It was such an emotional letter, but I am proud that I did it. It actually sounded like a rational adult instead of a hurt child, which is how I always imagined it would sound. I'm on my way to drop it off at the post office. And, I know that I am ready to face whatever happens, even if I never hear back." She carefully hands me the pen. "Thank you so much for sharing your mother's love with me. I truly felt like it brought out hidden love inside me that I didn't even know existed. What a good feeling!"

"You are more than welcome." I answer. "This pen certainly seems to have an effect. And, you just gave me a great idea! But I need to hurry in to shower and dress for lunch with the family. I really hope that it all works out with your mom!"

On the ride to lunch, Kyle notices my excitement. I fill him in on my conversation with Julie. "I can't wait to talk to Ella! She is getting ready to start writing the book, so I am taking the heart pen to her. She has been grappling with an ending for the story of my mother's love and the heart pen, and I have the perfect idea!"

We arrive at the house and Ella is sitting on the porch with her mom. Kyle starts talking to his mom, so I grab Ella to tell her that I have an ending. First, I fill her in on Julie's story. Then, I share my idea for the ending. "The pen will always have a temporary home in the shadow box with my mother's letter. But there will be times when a friend may need a little extra love. This pen may end up traveling many miles and to many people, carrying the magic of a mother's love with it." I say proudly.

Ella smiles as she adds, "A love that can provide confidence to reach for the stars or to search for true happiness."

We hug each other as I whisper, "It really is magical!"

EPILOGUE
20 YEARS LATER
LILY

Kyle and I still live in the same house. We have one daughter, Rose. You can guess how we came up with her name! She is 18 and is off enjoying her first semester at Florida State University. She moved into a dorm on campus, but at least she is close enough for frequent visits. Kyle still works at the same law firm. I left my job at the CPA firm to open my own tax practice. It was very scary to give up the security but has definitely proved to be the right decision. I have many clients and they are all like family to me!

Kathryn and Rick are still in Jacksonville. Their first child was a girl, named Sophie after my mother. They also had a son named Jack. They were never able to have any more children but were so thankful for these two who lit up their lives. Kathryn stayed true to her word by making them the best dressed kids ever! She dressed them in elaborate ensembles that were such a hit that she ended up starting her own line of clothes for children, called Kathryn's Kids. Her own kids served as models in the earlier years. Sophie is now in her second year at Florida State. She and Rose have always been the best of friends. Jack is 16 and stays quite busy with sports and high school.

Ella's first book became a best seller and was later made into a motion picture. She has written many other books, but none were quite as successful as her first. She met a fellow author at one of her book signings, who later became her husband. They are so cute together! They moved to the scenic mountains of North Carolina and live a quiet life as they continue to write.

Melody and Nikki Sue's song made it to #1 and remained at the top of the charts for seven months. They successfully opened their nonprofit, named Melodies, and have changed the lives of many, many young girls. Melody quit her professorship at FSU to take an active leadership role at Melodies. This requires lots of travel and she is loving the opportunity to help girls' groups all over the US. Some of the young girls have gone on to make careers out of their musical talents, and most all of them keep in touch with Melody.

Once Ella's book was published, more friends and acquaintances started asking to borrow the pen. It was passed around so much that it finally went missing about 10 years ago. I grieved over it for a while, then decided to imagine that love was following it everywhere. But, the empty spot in my shadow box always makes me a little sad. Will I ever see the heart pen again? I wonder...

About the author

Judi Taylor is retired and lives in The Villages, Florida with her husband. She worked as an accountant for a Fortune 500 company for twenty years, then owned a Jenny Craig Weight Loss Franchise. This is her first book. Judi's grandmother wrote a story about a mother's love. The handwritten story was later passed down to the family. It made such an impression, that Judi wanted to do the same. She can be reached at theheartpen@gmail.com

Made in the USA
Columbia, SC
19 September 2020